GREEN
THUMB

GREEN THUMB

RALPH McINERNY

 St. Martin's Minotaur ❦ New York

www.minotaurbooks.com

Library of Congress Cataloging-in-Publication Data

McInerny, Ralph M.
    Green thumb / Ralph McInerny.—1st ed.
      p. cm.
    ISBN 0-312-32419-7
    EAN 978-0312-32419-3
    1. Knight, Roger (Fictitious character)—Fiction. 2. Private investigators—Indiana—South Bend—Fiction. 3. Knight, Philip (Fictitious character)—Fiction. 4. College graduates—Crimes against—Fiction. 5. Philanthropists—Crimes against—Fiction. 6. University of Notre Dame—Fiction. 7. South Bend (Ind.)—Fiction. 8. College teachers—Fiction. 9. Brothers—Fiction. I. Title.

PS3563.A31166G74 2004
813'.54—dc22

2004046779

First Edition: November 2004

10 9 8 7 6 5 4 3 2 1

For Tom and Stacey Hibbs

PART ONE

1 GOLF CAN BE PLAYED AT ANY time of the day, but morning is best, the earlier the better. There are those who object to dew on the grass and to putted balls that elicit plumes of water from the greens, but they are to be pitied rather than blamed. In any case, God is merciful, and such tepid devotion is doubtless better than none. All the more reason to choose one's partners carefully lest a game be spoiled by the grousing of even one member of the group.

One June morning, Phil Knight stood on the first tee. From the trees and bushes came the twitter of birds he would not have presumed to identify, leaving that sort of thing to his brother, Roger. His ball sat high on its tee. He remained motionless over it for half a minute, took a final glance down the inviting vista of the fairway, then slowly drew back his club, brought it level to the ground behind his head, paused, and then in the descending swing shifted his weight slightly, keeping his head down. Club head met ball with a satisfying crack and his ball sailed out a hundred and fifty yards and rolled another twenty-five.

"Good shot, Phil."

Jimmy Stewart took his place on the tee and Phil got off to

the side, studying his grip on the driver, a mute suggestion that good as his drive had been, he was capable of better. Jimmy skied his ball and it plopped to a halt fifty yards out. Moments later the two men were in the cart, silently off for their second shots. Friends do not comment on a foozled shot, not simply as insurance against an inevitable bad shot of their own but in deference to the etiquette of the game. The golf course is the last bastion of courtesy in a declining civilization.

The Warren Golf Course is located on Douglas Road just east of the Notre Dame campus. It is the university course now but the old Burke course, nine holes of which still exist, is so heavy with bittersweet memories that for many Warren will never replace Burke. Phil Knight had no sentimental attachment to the old course. He and Roger had arrived in South Bend after Warren opened, but he sometimes played those surviving nine holes of Burke and could sympathize with those for whom Warren must forever be an imposter. Jimmy was one of them and thus it was that this morning it was Burke they played.

Like most natives of South Bend, Stewart considered himself an honorary alumnus. As a boy he had slipped over the fence separating the sixteenth fairway from Cedar Grove Cemetery and played the back holes out of sight of Rockne Memorial, which housed the clubhouse. When he returned from military service, he became a member of the South Bend police force that for years, before half of the old course had been cannibalized for new student residences, had played Burke every Tuesday evening in season, their tournament a gesture of gown to town. Mere words could not express his

4

feelings about the loss of the back nine of Burke to the encroachments of the new buildings. On this idyllic morning the two men were playing Burke because of an impending alumni tournament at Warren.

For his second shot Jimmy took a three wood and redeemed himself with a magnificent hit that landed on the green but then bounded to the right into a sand trap. The word he uttered was not a vulgarity under the circumstances but a mere statement of fact. Phil's seven iron scudded to the apron of the green and stopped. Of course, he said nothing about his good fortune.

Despite their different approaches, each man left the first green with a double bogie six and proceeded to the second hole. Whatever the fortunes of the game, the two friends were similarly affected by the peaceful setting, by the forgetfulness of all else that a golf course confers on its votaries, the vexations of the day left behind on the first tee. On the second green there were signs that someone had preceded them. Jimmy looked at Phil.

"He must have started by putting on the second," Jimmy said, his voice heavy with disapproval. The second green was separated from the first tee by a grassy declivity and a hedge.

"There he is."

Far off on the third fairway a solitary figure in a golf cart could be descried.

Phil shook his head. Was even golf to be affected by the lawlessness of the world?

By silent agreement the two men slowed their pace, not wanting to overtake the interloper ahead. The tracks of his

5

cart in the wet grass and his footprints on the greens, looking like dance steps, made it impossible to forget about him completely. When they came off the fifth green and went on to the next hole their slow pace was unrewarded: There was someone on the unmown sixth green. Six is a par three reachable by a nine iron or pitching wedge. Phil prudently took an eight iron from his bag and, having honors, teed up his ball. And waited.

"What's he doing?" Jimmy asked, disgust in his voice.

"Lining up his putt?"

The man was lying on the surface of the green and it was conceivable that he was seeking a better reading of the surface. But a minute passed and he remained lying where he was. Annoyance gave way to concern.

"I'll go see," Jimmy said.

"I'll come with you."

The holes behind them showed no signs as yet of other golfers. Jimmy was already behind the wheel of the cart and Phil slipped in beside him and they were off. Neither man spoke as they neared the green. There was little doubt that the man lying on the green had not moved since they first saw him. Jimmy pulled up behind the parked cart and jumped out, moving cautiously over the green. He was already crouched beside the man when Phil joined him.

"Dead?"

"Not quite. You got a phone with you, Phil?"

Phil nodded. He took his cell phone from his pocket and handed it to Jimmy, who dialed 911. The real world had intruded on their game.

2 ⟶ BEFORE THE POLICE CRUISERS
and the ambulance arrived, advancing
over the fairways with flashing lights, Jimmy scrutinized the
putting surface. His first instructions were that the green was
to be minutely photographed before the paramedics performed their necessary tasks. Phil grudgingly realized that
there would be no more golf that day. The photographer, in
bare feet, did as he was instructed, and then the body was
bagged and put into the ambulance. Jimmy drove the fallen
player's clubs and cart off for sequestration and then departed
in a police car still wearing his golf shoes. Phil directed his
cart back to the tee, retrieved his unhit ball, and headed in.

At the starting shed he paid Max, the attendant, who had
just arrived. Max was a squinty-eyed man whose knees kept
him from the game he loved. His only comfort now was to take
secret pleasure in the mishits of those still able to play,
remembering only the good drives he himself had hit in his
playing days. He was still staring, openmouthed, at the passage of the ambulance. "I thought it was you or Stewart," he
said solemnly.

"Not this time, Max."

"Was he playing with you?"

"He was ahead of us."

"Ahead!" Max squinted and rubbed his chin. "When did he start?"

There seemed no need to mention the way the fallen golfer had begun his round. It would be too much to regard what had happened to him as divine retribution but some such unformulated thought did cross Phil's mind. He carried his and Jimmy's clubs to the car in which both had arrived and drove to the apartment east of the library that he shared with his brother Roger. It was there, during a second breakfast—waffles and bacon and scrambled eggs—that Jimmy telephoned. Roger took the call.

"His name is Mortimer Sadler," Roger said, hanging up. "Or it was."

"Dead?"

"Dead."

Phil had given Roger an account of the interrupted round, not expecting his brother to understand what one was bound to think of a golfer who began a round by dropping a ball on the second green and putting out as if he had got there in the approved way.

"Sadler Hall," Roger said. This was one of the new residences built on the former back nine of the Burke golf course.

"Probably a coincidence."

Roger shook his head. "Mortimer Sadler."

A wave of sympathy passed through Phil. Had the man seen the building that his generosity had paid for and in an agony of remorse suffered a fatal stroke?

"May he rest in peace," Roger murmured.

"Amen," Phil said sincerely.

There are those who sneak a secret drink before a party. Mortimer Sadler was on campus for an irregular reunion of his class and might have gone out early on Burke as a kind of Sneaky Pete to ready himself for the later class tournament at Warren. This possibility brought back Phil's disapproval of the man and when Jimmy came by later he shared the sentiment.

"He was scheduled to tee off at Warren at nine-fifty-five."

Silence was sufficient comment.

"He must have loved golf," Roger said.

The silence deepened.

An hour later Father Carmody arrived. He had spent the morning at the new golf course, fraternizing with returned alumni, speaking with Toolin, and reliving his glory days when he had been a mover and shaker behind the scenes at Notre Dame. One of his last accomplishments had been to bring Roger Knight to campus as the Huneker Professor of Catholic Studies, a position that gave Roger unusual autonomy, being attached to no particular department but having his classes listed in several. Among other things, he was spending the summer preparing a course on the revival of Catholic literature in France in the late nineteenth and early twentieth centuries. This was the initial topic of conversation when the priest arrived.

"No course on Huneker?"

Father Carmody had long urged Roger to offer a course devoted to the writings of the man after whom his endowed professorship was named, but studying those writings had dulled any enthusiasm Roger had first expressed.

"Not this semester."

"The donors would like it," Carmody said softly.

"Have you read Huneker, Father?"

"Not a word. I will sit in on the course when you give it."

"Sadler was a donor," Roger said, to redirect the conversation.

"You couldn't give a course on him."

"Did you know him?"

Is the pope Polish? In the manner of the old, when short-term memory is unreliable, Father Carmody retained an encyclopedic mental hard drive on the young men who had gone through the university during his active years. Some young women, too, but Father Carmody's Notre Dame was still that of Richard Sullivan's affectionate memoir of the university, published in 1951. Of course he knew Mortimer Sadler.

"Dreadful man. Dreadful boy, for that matter."

"Tell us about him."

Mortimer Sadler, class of 1977, had been an undergraduate during the first generation of women students at Notre Dame. In a flamboyant column he had written for *The Observer,* he had embarked on a veritable crusade, writing again and again that the university had made a mistake in going coeducational. His misogyny stemmed in large part from the indifference those women students showed to his efforts to acquaint them with the marvels of the Mortimer Sadler personality. It should be said that the first women admitted to Notre Dame were the crème de la crème, most of them valedictorians of their high school classes, as a group more gifted than the male students. Mortimer had never excelled as a student, considering his four years at Notre Dame to be a preparation not for the intellectual life but for the career in business for which he was destined. He was the scion of the Sadler family of Minneapolis, who had prospered in insurance as a robust belief in providence waned.

"I once suggested that he could be related to the writer," Father Carmody said.

"The writer?"

"Mary Anne Sadlier."

"Despite the altered spelling?"

Father Carmody ignored the question. The point was that Roger now recognized the Catholic woman author to whom he referred.

"He reacted as if I had suggested a female ancestor had been a woman of loose morals."

"A prude?"

"About the life of the mind. He brought home to one the fact that athletic *fan* derives from *fanatic*. I was prompted to make the suggestion about Sadlier when Mortimer wrote a story, a fantasy of the future when the Notre Dame football team would be coed."

"Was it any good?"

"It was horrible. Have you read Mary Anne Sadlier?"

"Not yet."

The conversation turned to what Jimmy Stewart had

11

learned at the hospital. The supposition that Sadler had been felled by a stroke had been dismissed and the family by telephone had agreed to an autopsy.

"He paid for one of the new halls," Father Carmody said.

"He was wealthy?"

"Reasonably so."

Once Sadler would have been thought a veritable Croesus among donors, but nowadays Notre Dame was the beneficiary of men of unimaginable riches, not all of them alumni. Not all of them Catholics, either, but for many the university had become an emotional tie with a lost faith. Its prosperity attracted ever more generosity, and those who had known great success in the world took inordinate pleasure in having their names attached to campus buildings.

"Once we named residences after former presidents or great priests like John A. Zahm. And Rockne, of course."

The priest's voice became wistful as he remembered those better days.

"Who ever thought there would be a residence named after Mortimer Sadler? But God is not mocked."

"What do you mean?"

"It is a women's residence."

3　WHEN MORTIMER SADLER FAILED to show up at his scheduled teeoff time at Warren, the three men who had been anxiously awaiting his arrival drove off without him. Unhappily. Reduced to a threesome they were ineligible for the prizes reserved for foursomes, such as the greatest number of putts. There was a prize for the least number as well, but these men were realists and put their hope neither in princes nor in their athletic skills.

"Mort is usually the first one on the tee," Ben Barley said to Jim Crown, with whom he shared a cart. The third member of the group, Chris Toolin, had a cart to himself.

"I phoned his room," Ben added. "No answer."

"Phoned?"

Ben patted the cell phone in a holster on his belt. Chris scowled. Much of his wealth came from investments in telecommunications, but he would cheerfully abolish the cell phone if he could. How many inane conversations had he been made privy to while exhibitionists broadcast their supposed private conversations to the ambient world? Chris remembered the dark day when, napping in the VIP lounge of an airport, a shrill woman's voice behind him brought him abruptly awake. She spoke loudly; she seemed to be addressing him, and he turned in alarm. She ignored him and went on speaking into the instrument she held. Dear God. A monument should be raised to the man who invented the phone booth. Perhaps legislation could be introduced requiring that the use of cell phones be confined to booths. But no. Too much legislation was on the books already. In political theory, Chris Toolin was a species of libertarian, but when he exalted freedom he was thinking largely of his own. Who knew, someday he, too, might have need of a cell phone.

"No answer."

"I thought he must be out early, practicing."

"But we agreed to no prior practicing."

"And a mulligan off the first tee." Crown had availed himself of that privilege when his first drive went abruptly south after heading out toward the fairway.

Ben Barley, Crown, Toolin, and Sadler had all shared a quad in St. Edward's Hall as undergraduates, and they were acquainted with all the flaws in his character, as he was with theirs. It was perfectly conceivable to them that Mort, after solemnly agreeing to the no-prior-practice rule, would have got to the course early like the big bad wolf and hit a bucket of balls to limber up. But all efforts to locate Mort as their tee time approached had proved futile. If he had been on the course he would have been found.

"Dead in bed?" Crown suggested.

Ben made the sign of the cross. The old classmates had reached the half-century mark and most days still felt in the full vigor of youth. Nonetheless, from time to time, one of their classmates died. Forty of their class had died already. As an

14

insurance man, Mort would have known the statistical unlikelihood of that happening to any of them.

"More likely hung over."

Crown smiled. Last night the foursome had dined at the Morris Inn, where they were staying, gone on to the bar afterward, and from thence to the suite Mort was writing off as a business expense, a large corner room from which the bedroom was separated by what Barley called a distinction of reason.

"A what?"

"Don't get him started."

Whenever Ben Barley returned to campus whole lectures came back to him that he had not thought of for years. He was particularly susceptible to remembered philosophy courses. He had majored in theology and mathematics, unsure whether he had a vocation to the priesthood or to high school teaching. In any event, he became a lawyer in Chicago.

"It's funny, when I come down for games it doesn't happen. I think I have to be with you guys. Do you remember the Principle of Sufficient Reason?"

A pillow thrown from across the room silenced him. There followed ten minutes of the kind of mayhem that had characterized their undergraduate life: cushions torn from the couch and used as chest protectors, bottles of tonic water turned into weapons with which to spray others. Crown, remembering a bit of Latin before the liturgical reforms unleashed by Vatican II, intoned the *Asperges me hyssopo* when he shook his bottle and then, with its mouth half covered by the ball of his thumb, directed a spray of tonic water in a wide arc. A lamp was overturned, a chair upended, shouts and laughter filled the room. When the activity subsided, they collapsed on the floor wherever they had stood, filled with fierce and false memories of carefree youth.

"More likely," Ben agreed. "How's your head?"

"Don't ask."

The two men took their second shots and drove on to where Chris awaited them beside his drive. Chris was the only one of the four who golfed well and he professed to prefer tennis. But then he played every game well. Effortlessly. He had done well producing infomercials for cable television channels, a once promising creativity directed into lucrative if trivial pursuits. Once he himself as well as the others had expected great things from him in the literary line. But the competent short stories of his undergraduate days had not proved a prelude to anything more. The previous night he had announced his attention to write a book called *Ventriloquism for Dummies*. All had laughed and then fallen silent, as if commemorating the death of his promise.

Toolin, Crown, Barley, and Sadler. The four had kept in desultory touch since graduation. It had been Sadler who convinced a significant number of the class to defy the alumni association and hold their class reunion apart from the five-year intervals that brought other classes back to the campus for bouts of nostalgia. So it was that thirty-five members of the class of 1977 had reserved rooms in the Morris Inn and returned for two days of togetherness at Notre Dame. Paths that had diverged briefly converged and their practice had received the eventual benediction of the alumni association, thereby removing some of the zest from their reunions. Since he had been the initiator, Mort retained the right to devise the schedule of these days. The golf tournament on the second and final day had become de rigueur, looked forward to throughout the year by Mort, who could not abandon his undergraduate dream of athletic prowess. He bought the instructional videos advertised in Toolin's infomericals, he sent off for trick clubs and devices guaranteed to improve his swing, and he was coached weekly by a pro in Minneapolis. And his game improved—so long as he did not play at Notre Dame. Returning to the campus brought back all the ineptitude of his undergraduate days and the faults that had been overcome in Minneapolis returned with a vengeance in South Bend. His old friends were right to suspect that he had stolen some time to practice before the scheduled match, despite previous agreements made with less than clear minds the night before. Perhaps he considered that playing a few holes on the old course did not violate the agreement, though none of his friends would have suspected him of such scrupulosity.

"Maybe he ran away with Maureen O'Kelly," Barley suggested on the first green, speaking while Toolin was in the act of putting.

Crown barked with laughter. Toolin's ball rolled twenty feet past the hole.

Since the renunion was Mort Sadler's inspiration, it was boycotted by the women in their class.

"Girlcotted?" Barley asked. A return to Notre Dame brought back facetiousness like a plague.

Maureen O'Kelly had taken a room in the Morris Inn as a

17

member of the reunion, accompanied by Francie, her eldest daughter. When Mort had been sent the list of registrants by the Morris Inn he had immediately phoned his old roommates to inform them of the outrage.

"She's a member of the class, Mort."

"Wasn't she our valedictorian?"

As if anyone could forget the commencement at which Maureen had harangued the twelve thousand people gathered in the Joyce Center for their graduation. Maureen had recalled the campaign carried on in *The Observer* without mentioning Mortimer Sadler by name, but of course every student there knew to whom she referred. Mortimer had sat sweating through the ordeal, which was made worse by his remembering the jocular incredulity with which Maureen had greeted his advances during their freshman year. Her disdainful dismissal of his suit had been the origin of his campaign against coeducation at Notre Dame. And now, on the culminating day of their four-year stay, she was allowed to malign him without possibility of reply. He had seethed. He had seethed during the years since whenever he recalled that ignominious occasion. And now she was registered in the Morris Inn, brazenly present at the reunion that had hitherto attracted only males of the class.

"I understand the poor woman is a widow."

"Only a trial separation. And she is not a poor woman. She is amply provided for."

"She is more beautiful now than when she was young."

This was the unkindest cut of all, because it was so manifestly true. The previous night, before the golf tournament, when the four old roommates—they had presumed to refer to themselves as the Four Horsemen but dropped it when others called them the Four Jockeys—were dining in Sorin's Restaurant at the inn, Maureen had come to their table. Her luxuriant hair was still golden, her features might have adorned the cover of a fashion magazine, her green eyes were playful as she stood over them.

"Ah, the chauvinists reunited."

This accusation was vigorously protested by Mortimer's three friends. Barley assured Maureen that they had had nothing to do with Mortimer's quixotic campaign.

"But you never repudiated it."

"We do so now," Barely assured her, and two other heads nodded assent. During this exchange, Maureen had studiously avoided looking at Mortimer, who sat transfixed by her beauty as he vainly sought some word of repartee that would destroy her superiority.

"Let bygones be bygones," Toolin said. "After all, you have come."

"My daughter Francie and I are looking forward to the tournament. She was runner-up for the state amateur championship in Minnesota."

"How is your game?"

"Not quite as good as hers."

"Are you willing to wager on it?" Mortimer managed to say.

"Wager what?"

"My score against yours."

"What is your handicap?"

"Seventeen."

She laughed. "Think of all the strokes I'll have to give you."

But the offer had been made and was heartily endorsed by Mortimer's companions. The bet was for a hundred dollars. Belatedly, Mortimer remembered that Maureen had won the women's golf tournament during their commencement week. Even with the strokes she apparently had to give him, he was uncertain that he could beat her.

"What is your handicap, Maureen?"

"The memory of an elephant." And her green eyes burned into Mortimer's uplifted face. "See you on the course."

She walked away, and her graceful movements were followed with murmuring approval from Mortimer's table companions. He had walked into a trap. Maureen would beat him tomorrow, and it would stand as the refutation of everything he had written in *The Observer*.

"She won't stay single long," Barley said.

"Her daughter is a lovely girl."

All this was dust and ashes to Mortimer and he was unable to conceal it, thus opening himself to the teasing of his old friends. He sought consolation in drink and later, during the horseplay in his suite, he seemed to have forgotten the episode. But he was filled with foreboding. What if his golfing skills should desert him again when he played on campus?

Thus it was that his three old friends concluded that a fearful Mortimer had gone out to play some practice holes on

Burke before teeing up on Warren. Perhaps he would have been felled on the latter course, but there his death would not have been tainted with dishonor from breaking his promise about practicing to his old friends. Everyone assumed it was a stroke that killed him.

4 MORTIMER SADLER'S DEATH HAD been caused by poison.

"Poison!" Roger said when he took Jimmy Stewart's call and was informed of the result of the autopsy.

"Deadly nightshade."

"Good Lord. How in the world . . ."

"That's what we have to find out."

Roger looked up deadly nightshade on the Google Web site and printed out a lengthy entry. After glancing through it, he put it aside. Roger was now reading the critical essays of Barbey d'Aurevilly, moving systematically through the volumes that filled a shelf on the eighth floor of the Hesburgh Library. He found it difficult to concentrate in light of what had happened to Mortimer Sadler—difficult, not impossible. But while he read, half his brain was pondering what he had heard from Jimmy Stewart. No one seeing him smiling as he turned the pages of the book would imagine that he was also thinking of the death that had occurred that morning on the sixth green of the old golf course.

But Phil was not deceived. Meanwhile he went downtown to be of such assistance as he could to Stewart, having received a call from Father Carmody.

"Philip, I am authorized to engage your services to represent the best interests of the university during the investigation into Mortimer Sadler's death."

"It is now thought that he was poisoned."

"Well, he had a poison pen."

Whatever the priest's intention, the remark suggested that Sadler's death was somehow linked to his undergraduate journalism. Greg Whelan had come for lunch, while they were awaiting the autopsy report, and told them of Sadler's constant ranting about coeducation in his columns in *The Observer*. Greg had read them all, but then he seemed to have read everything contained in the university archives, where he was an associate director.

"Did he think the university would revoke the policy?"

"He argued that they should. Of course he knew he was embarked on a losing campaign. It added zest to his style."

Jimmy welcomed Phil's cooperation. "It should smooth our way on campus. There are all kinds of people I must talk to before they leave."

"His former classmates?"

"Thirty-five or so are here for the reunion he organized."

The tournament at Warren went on as scheduled, and Maureen had the fifth-lowest score. She dismissed the suggestion that, as the top woman golfer, she should receive a trophy. Her daughter had outscored Maureen but, of course, she was not entered in the tournament. She was in the class of 2005 at St. Mary's, her loveliness reminiscent of her mother as a girl. The former roommates of St. Edward's Hall were married, one and all, but it would have taken a St. Anthony of the desert to have been unmoved by the beauty of mother and daughter. The beads of sweat on their foreheads, pale thanks to the sunshades they had worn, and their damp golden hair enhanced rather than detracted from their beauty.

"Like mother, like daughter," Toolin said, and sighed.

Barley had been on the phone to the Morris Inn and returned with the alarming news. Mortimer Sadler had been taken by ambulance from the old course and was pronounced dead when he arrived at the hospital.

"Dead!"

The inevitability of death in general does not diminish its surprise in the individual case, but this was a man of their own age, one they had known when young, a man with whom they had drunk and cavorted the previous night. This was not the time to comment on the perfidy that had taken him out on the old course at the crack of dawn in the wan hope of acquiring a competitive advantage for the tournament that lay ahead.

"It was the bet with Maureen that undid him," Toolin nevertheless decided.

It was only when showered, restored with a drink in the clubhouse, and returned to the Morris Inn, that they learned the manner of Mortimer's death.

"Poison!"

"What a way to go."

"Why did he do it?"

" 'Do it'?"

24

"It's obvious, isn't it? He couldn't face the prospect of being beaten by the beautiful Maureen."

"She can beat me anytime," Crown said equivocally.

The remark fell like an obscenity uttered in church.

"Poor Mort."

"May he rest in peace."

"Amen."

5   ➤   CAL SWITHINS HAD BEEN LET GO
by *The South Bend Tribune* but contin-
ued to regard himself as a reporter, however he was regarded
by others. He wrote a column for a shopping guide that was
flung free at doorsteps in the city and stuffed with other
unwanted materials into curbside mailboxes in the suburbs.
The fuzzy photograph that accompanied these efforts—
"Swithins Sez"—was a reasonable likeness of himself twenty
years before. Time had taken its toll since then, time and the
disappointments and reversals that had characterized his
journalistic career. To himself, Swithins explained the fact
that no one had ever mentioned the column to him as a result
of that imperfect likeness. The title of the column had been
chosen by the editor and publisher, Maddie Yost, whose late
husband had founded *The Shopper*. She had come into sole
possession of it some years before when her husband had
gone off a country road and totaled the family car in a colli-
sion with a sturdy oak.

" 'Swithins Sez'?"

"It's catchy."

"It's corny."

"Of course it's corny. That's the point."

He ended by being grateful for the out-of-date photo that accompanied his animadversions.

"Don't use no words like that on this paper."

He promised to restrict his style to monosyllables and unadorned declarative sentences. Maddie ignored this grammatical lore.

"It's just filler anyway."

With what she paid him, it was a licence to starve as well. Not that Maddie thought of him as a columnist. His main task, in her eyes, was to drum up new advertisers for the paper. Of course, he had other arrows in his quiver as well. He did piecework for the newspaper that had fired him, writing the death notices as well as unsigned accounts of Little League baseball in season. His application for employment was on file in the Office of Human Resources at Notre Dame. He longed to be taken on by one of the campus publications, where the pay was allegedly regal and the work risible. From time to time, he wrote critiques of these publications and dropped them off at the relevant offices, showing the flag. With the passage of years, he had begun to doubt that he would ever become a university employee. This was added to his list of grievances. In his rented room on South Main he had a little stuffed leprechaun, picked up at the Hammes Bookstore on campus. He used it as a pincushion whenever he unwrapped a new shirt, muttering what might have seemed curses as he plunged them in.

But his long run of bad luck had not induced despair. Despite it all, hope sprang, if not eternal then at least intermittently, in Swithins's breast. He lived on the alert for the big chance. When he heard of the death on the Notre Dame golf course something told him not to ask for whom this bell tolled.

One of the advantages of having a persona that did not attract attention—sometimes Swithins thought he had become the invisible man, so thoroughly was he ignored—was that he could loll around the press room at police headquarters and keep au courant without being noticed. It was there that he heard the death of Mortimer Sadler mentioned. Swithins looked at the speaker, Raskow, a dissolute overweight veteran of the press who affected an unlit cigar and wide-brimmed felt hat, the better to cover his absence of hair. Raskow clearly did not see the significance of what he said.

Swithins rose and went unnoticed out the door and down the hall to the office of Jimmy Stewart. There was a tall stranger with him. Their conversation stopped when Swithins stood in the doorway.

"What can you tell me about Mortimer Sadler?"

"I don't remember your name."

"Calvin Swithins. I'm a reporter."

"I thought you left town."

"I'm back."

"I'll be making a statement to the press later."

But Swithins had put two and two together. If Jimmy Stewart was interested in Sadler's death, homicide must be involved.

"How was the murder accomplished?"

"Murder?"

"You're in homicide, aren't you?"

Stewart was annoyed, but then he was used to dealing with such domesticated animals as Raskow.

"Come to the press conference later. You back with the *Tribune*?"

"I never left." Swithins hitched up his belt. "I do the obituaries."

Stewart relaxed. This wasn't lost on Swithins. He should have used this earlier. Stewart was clearly relieved to conclude that Swithins's only interest in the death of Mortimer Sadler was to write his death notice. This, he decided, would be his cover as he investigated the matter. Already he was certain that the death of Mortimer Sadler was his ticket to fame and fortune.

"This a new man?" Swithins asked, indicating the stranger.

"I'm Philip Knight," the tall man said, hesitating, then giving Swithins his hand.

If Swithins had been a pinball machine he would have lit up on learning that this was the private detective whose brother was now a member of the faculty of Notre Dame. Knight had teamed with Jimmy Stewart on other campus investigations.

"You can probably find what you need on campus," Knight said.

"Good idea."

"Try the Alumni Office in the Eck Center."

Swithins dutifully left, going out to his car. He was still seated behind the wheel, plotting his strategy, when a car emerged from the police garage, Stewart at the wheel, Knight in the passenger seat beside him.

He got his car started on the second try and pulled away from the curb, keeping the unmarked police car in sight.

6 → THE MEMBERS OF THE CLASS OF
'77 had been asked to delay their depar-
ture plans, but after preliminary questioning this seemed an
unnecessary hardship. In the end, only Sadler's former roommates were asked to stay. Maureen O'Kelly and her daughter
Francie had booked into the Morris Inn for a week. It occurred
to Jimmy Stewart that he and Phil Knight knew as much of the
circumstances of Sadler's death as anyone else, having been
on the course when he died.

Max, the starter, in response to instructions from Stewart,
had taken possession of Sadler's golf clubs, driving the cart to
which they were strapped into the maintenance shed and
posting a DO NOT TOUCH sign on its windshield. Cart and clubs
were taken away to the police lab shortly after noon. Meanwhile, Jimmy, with Phil at his side, talked with Sadler's former roommates.

Chris Toolin asked to be first, as he had an appointment in
Chicago the following afternoon. Had Sadler given any indication that his life was in danger?

"Wasn't it suicide?"

"Why would you think so?"

"Who else would do it?"

"He had no enemies?"

"Of course there were people who didn't like him, people who didn't know him as well as I did. He held pretty strong opinions and wasn't shy about expressing them."

"About what?"

"About everything. I don't know about any of his associates in Minneapolis, but no one on campus would do such a thing."

"Well, he's dead."

"Why have you excluded suicide?"

"We haven't."

Toolin seemed to review the conversation thus far to see if this was true. He accepted Stewart's disclaimer.

"What kind of poison was it?"

"Deadly nightshade."

"Sounds like a lethal window blind."

"It's lethal, all right."

"Where can it be obtained?"

"We're looking into that."

"Mort wouldn't know a nightshade from a venetian blind."

"Was he despondent, down, sad?"

"You should have been at our celebration last night." Toolin smiled. His smile faded. "He did make a silly bet on today's match."

And so they heard of the appearance of Maureen O'Kelly at their table in the dining room.

"Why would he make such a bet with her?"

"It's a long story."

"We've got time."

Toolin glanced at his watch. "Coeducation began the year before we entered Notre Dame. Mortimer Sadler became a big foe of it, writing all kinds of articles in *The Observer*, urging the university to return to its traditional status as an all-male institution."

"Didn't he like girls?"

Toolin tried not to smile. "They didn't like him. In freshman year he made a big play for Maureen. She just made fun of him. His luck continued bad. Then he began his crusade against coeducation."

"A male scorned?" Phil asked.

Toolin nodded. "This was all a long time ago."

"Is he married?"

"Married? He has four children."

"Good Lord."

"All girls. He wouldn't let them enroll here. Sent them all to St. Mary's." His mouth dropped. "Have they been told?"

"They might want to talk to an old friend of his."

"My God, I'd rather not."

Jimmy had already called Minneapolis and told Mrs. Sadler that she was now a widow. Not that bluntly, of course, but there was no way the news he had to give could be softened. Nor was the task made easier by the suggestion that an autopsy be conducted. Patricia Sadler tearfully agreed and said she would be on the first available flight to South Bend.

"Northwest has a direct flight," she added, and gave a little sob. "I know because Mort took it. The kids can drive down."

32

Jim Crown knew a good deal of Sadler's life in Minneapolis, which he visited often from Rochester, where he was on the staff of the Mayo Clinic.

"That's out of Agatha Christie," he said when told of the deadly nightshade.

"Have you had any experience of it?"

"Only in bad fiction."

"Who might have poisoned him?"

"No one among his business associates. He was the toast of Minneapolis. Here at Notre Dame he had a reputation for controversy, but I think he left that behind at graduation."

"Domestic life all right?"

"He has four kids. He and Pat are like honeymooners."

"Jackie Gleason."

"That was before my time."

"Mine too."

Crown held up a hand. "You know, when Mort was an undergraduate he once made himself sick to avoid an exam. He nearly killed himself. Accidentally. What was it he took?" Crown tried to recall but could not. "What if he was trying to get out of the tournament and the bet with Maureen O'Kelly and he accidentally killed himself?"

"Had he ever tried anything like that since he was a student?"

"Lieutenant, you have to remember what coming back here does. It doesn't much matter what you have done since graduation—being on campus restores the persona you had here.

It's as if the experience of a lifetime is erased and you're just a stupid kid again. You should have seen the four of us romping last night."

Ben Barley's eyes were red from crying. His was the first real emotion Jimmy and Phil had encountered among Sadler's old friends.

"The poor sonofagun." Barley dabbed at his eyes. "The only comfort is that he died at Notre Dame."

"Did he want that?"

Barley stared. "Who wouldn't? Gentlemen, this is a special place. You have to be an alumnus to understand."

"Would he have killed himself in order to die here?"

"Suicide? A mortal sin? Not on your life. Mortimer Sadler was an outstanding Catholic, a true son of Notre Dame."

"I understand he didn't like the daughters of Notre Dame."

Barley made a face. "That was long ago."

"Someone said that coming back to campus turns you into an undergraduate again, or words to that effect."

Barley nodded thoughtfully. "That's true. Up to a point."

"How about the bet with Mrs. O'Kelly?"

"You don't think that she. . . ?"

"Why would we think that?"

"What you said. She hated Mort's guts. Have you heard of the talk she gave at commencement?"

"Tell us about it."

"She really took after Mort in it. Before thousands of people. Not by name, of course, but we knew he was the target."

"Why was she speaking at commencement?"

"She was valedictorian."

"Smart?"

Barley closed his eyes and whistled softly. "Brilliant. And she was as beautiful then as she is now."

"She stopped by your table in the dining room last night."

"So you've been told of that."

"Isn't that when the bet was made?"

"I don't think either of them was serious."

After talking with Barley, Jimmy decided to take a break and they went into the bar for a beer. Sitting at a little table, looking out at the greenery, they reviewed what they had learned. It didn't help much. Then Jimmy called in. He held the phone to his ear, his face impassive. He turned off the phone and looked at Phil.

"The poison was in his water bottle."

7 FRANCIE O'KELLY HAD AGREED TO accompany her mother on this grudge return to Notre Dame but her motive, of course, was otherwise. She would be a senior at St. Mary's across the way and had an ambivalent attitude toward the larger institution. St. Mary's continued as a women's college, having successfully resisted the blandishments of Notre Dame to merge. It was the failure of that effort at uniting the two institutions that had led to Notre Dame's decision to go coed. At the time, this had been thought vindictive since the supposition was that if women could go to Notre Dame, they would eschew St. Mary's and the college would wither on the vine. In any event, the college flourished. Its students had all the advantages of the facilities at Notre Dame while retaining the repose and dignity of a women's institution. Despite the presence of so many eligible women on the Notre Dame campus, perhaps because of it, the women of St. Mary's continued to be favored by Notre Dame men. Thus it was that Francie and Paul Sadler had met and entered upon a stormy but unbreakable relationship. This trip to South Bend with her mother gave Francie the opportunity of seeing Paul, who was taking a summer course in botany and working with the golf sports camp, the position secured by the fact that he was a member of the golf team.

"How was your game?"

"Okay."

"Beat your mother?"

"Of course."

"Come on, she's good."

Francie dipped her head in acknowledgment of this. She herself golfed well because she didn't take the game seriously, and it still surprised her that intelligent people like Paul and her mother could consider knocking a ball about and rolling it into a hole as an accomplishment to be boasted of. ESPN carried matches in strange sports, and trying to follow them brought home to her the idiocy of most games. Francie was wise enough to keep such heresy to herself. With Paul she was willing to talk golf until the cows came home.

"How about tonight?"

"I promised my mother to have dinner with her. Want to join us?"

"Where?"

"The Morris Inn."

He shook his head. "My uncle is staying there."

This was the notorious Mortimer Sadler, her mother's nemesis, bête noire, and designated Hittite. Paul seemed scarcely more fond of his uncle than did Maureen O'Kelly.

"What's he ever done to you?" she had asked the first time Paul made a face at the mention of his uncle Mortimer.

"It's a family thing."

"Oh well . . ."

"It would bore you."

"I'll be the judge of that."

There were four Sadler siblings: two sons, Mortimer and Paul's father, Samuel, who was a few years older; and the two girls, Bridget and Irene, both younger. They had married and moved away from Minneapolis, but by the terms of their father's will the four were equal heirs to the fortune he had amassed. They not only owned equal shares in the Sadler insurance agency, the four were on the board of governors of the Sadler Foundation. Mortimer was president of both the agency and the foundation because Samuel had no head for business. Paul had been raised in Deephaven, the youngest of three, and when he went off to Notre Dame his widowed father sold the house and bought a cabin on an isolated shore of Lake Minnetonka.

"What does he do?"

"He reads a lot. He's stopped playing golf."

Paul made this sound like his epitaph, but Sam Sadler's health was good. He had taught philosophy in a local community college on the strength of a doctorate from Tulane, gained after his graduation from Notre Dame. He had taken early retirement.

"He spent his life teaching. Now he says he wants to educate himself."

"I'd love to meet him."

"No, you wouldn't."

"Why not?"

"He'll talk philosophy to you."

It sounded like heaven. Francie had been smitten by the Socratic dialogues in her freshman year and had taken a philosophy course every semester since. She wondered if Paul, too, might mature into the man he described his father as being.

"It's too bad about the golf," she said diplomatically.

"Tragic. He always beat me when we played."

"Are you sure you didn't let him beat you?"

Paul was shocked. The point of golf was to score lower than your opponent, whoever it was. The thought that he might ease up out of deference to his father was incomprehensible.

Whatever Paul's future potential, she had to face the fact that right now he was a jock—a student athlete, in the phrase, for whom classes were a nuisance. Nonetheless, she had tried to interest him in Roger Knight.

One of the perks of the St. Mary's student is the ability to enroll in courses at Notre Dame—and vice versa, of course, though the traffic was largely in one direction. Thus it was that Francie had discovered Roger Knight, the Huneker Professor of Catholic Studies, drawn to a course titled "Descartes As Catholic Author." From the first day she had been enthralled. They had discussed Maritain's *The Dream of Descartes* and the evidence that Descartes had kept his vow to make a pilgrimage to the House of Loreto in gratitude for the philosophical revelation vouchsafed him in a dream. The account of this dream, which Roger Knight compared in some detail to the Memorial of Pascal, has not survived, but the philosopher had it with him when he died in Stockholm. The fact that none of this interested Paul had put a severe strain on their friendship, which nearly did not survive in their junior year.

"Give me plants any day."

"Plants?"

"I'm taking botany."

Francie said nothing, assuming it was a jock course, an easy C or even B for student athletes, not too demanding. But Paul had followed it up with others, so maybe it wasn't just easy credits.

Paul was only one of the targets of opportunity that had brought Francie to campus with her mother. The other was Roger Knight.

8 AFTER RECEIVING HIS DOCTOR-
ate in philosophy from Princeton, Roger
Knight, obese, eccentric, and brilliant, had found himself to
be academically unemployable. A lesser man might have
repined and lamented his fate, but Roger almost welcomed it.
Learning had never been pursued by him with a utilitarian
purpose—future employment—but for its own sake, and
nothing in his depressed circumstances prevented him from
continuing that pursuit. And continue it he did, a freelancer
in the world of scholarship, in contact via e-mail with like-
minded souls around the world, pursuing now one spoor of his
interests and now another. His brother, Philip, a private
detective, had after suffering his second mugging decided to
absent himself from felicity awhile and moved from Manhattan up the Hudson to Rye. He placed ads in the yellow pages
of various telephone directories around the country, identifiable only by profession and an 800 number, and accepted
such employment as promised unusual reward. Eventually,
Roger, who accompanied Phil when he accepted a client,
himself applied for and received a private detective licence.
And so their life might have continued if Roger's monograph
on the English writer who styled himself Baron Corvo had not

enjoyed an unforeseen success. Roger had become a Catholic while at Princeton and was drawn toward the study of such unusual subjects as Corvo, whose real name, insofar as reality applied to him, was Frederick Rolfe. The monograph had attracted the attention of Father Carmody, and he proposed to the donor of the Huneker Chair of Catholic Studies that Roger be installed in the professorship at Notre Dame. This had been done against the usual opposition, and for some years now the Knight brothers had pursued their common and separate interests at South Bend. For Phil, access to the year-round athletic program at Notre Dame was a kind of nirvana, for Roger the opportunity to offer courses in whatever interest currently engaged him was welcome, and he had at his fingertips a magnificent library, to say nothing of the university archives. From time to time, as in the case of the death of Mortimer Sadler, Phil was asked to function in his all-but-abandoned professional capacity.

"Suicide has been excluded, Phil?"

"Not excluded. But he showed none of the symptoms of one about to take his own life. The idea that he killed himself to avoid losing a bet to Maureen O'Kelly is ridiculous."

"What poison was involved?"

"Deadly nightshade."

"Belladonna," Roger murmured.

"Deadly nightshade."

"It has several names. Devil's cherries. Naughty man's cherries. Devil's herb. Others."

"Cherries?"

"The berry of the plant can be lethal. So can the leaves and root."

"It was introduced into the water bottle from which he drank on his final round of golf."

Of course Phil had given Roger an account of his early-morning round with Jimmy Stewart, the South Bend detective lieutenant with whom the brothers had formed a friendship in previous joint endeavors. The account was slowed by Phil's describing every stroke he and Jimmy had taken before arriving on the sixth tee.

"He was lying on the green?"

"This did not surprise us at first. Any man who had started a round in the way he had was capable of anything. We thought he was lining up his putt. It was when he didn't move that we went to investigate."

Roger was fascinated by the story of the irregular meetings of the class of 1977 under the inspiration of the dead golfer.

"The three men with whom he had shared rooms as an undergraduate are also here, and they celebrated the night before in Sadler's suite at the Morris Inn."

"No indication of what lay ahead?"

"None."

"So what do you think?"

"On the basis of what we know, I don't know what to think. It is conceivable that he committed suicide, planning the deed so that it occurred on a final round on the course he would have played as an undergraduate. But, as I said, his old friends saw no signs of such an intention. And there was no note."

"He does not sound like a suicidal type—insofar as there is one."

"And then, of course, there is Maureen O'Kelly."

"O'Kelly!"

Listening to Phil's account of the lone female member of the class of 1977 who had shown up for the irregular reunion, Roger of course thought at once of Francie.

Professors with more experience than Roger's are perhaps less surprised by a combination of striking beauty and exceptional mental gifts. An old bachelor like his brother, Roger nonetheless was capable of recognizing beauty when he saw it, and the first time Francie had come to ask permission to register for one of his courses he had realized that she was worthy of a Renaissance painter.

"Permission?"

"You must realize how difficult it is to enroll in one of your courses."

"Nonsense."

"There is an upper limit of fifteen and it has already been exceeded."

"So we will exceed it by one more."

"I will need a note from you."

"You shall have one."

It was not her beauty alone that won him; if he had been that susceptible he might no longer be a bachelor, despite his avoirdupois and eccentricity. And he had noticed that his clumsy obesity brought out a motherly impulse in coeds. But before offering to write the note he had asked Francie what her interest in Claudel was.

"Have you read him?" he asked.

"Only the *Journals*."

"The *Journals*." They were untranslated.

"I found a two-volume edition in the Bibliothèque de la Pléiade and bought them on an impulse. I find them fascinating."

"In what way?"

"All the biblical references."

"You read Latin?" Claudel always cited the Bible in Latin.

"Well enough."

So he told her that Claudel had a copy of the Vulgate Bible on his desk throughout his long diplomatic career and that, in retirement, he had devoted himself exclusively to writing commentaries on Scripture.

"He deplored modern biblical criticism and the foundation of the Ecole Biblique in Jerusalem. His contention was that only a poet could understand the Old Testament."

"Will you be talking of his biblical commentaries?"

"Of little else. Does that interest you?"

Her enthusiasm was clearly genuine. That was when he resolved to smooth her way into his class. It would have been a species of crime to keep her out of it; he saw that more and more as the semester proceeded. He put her onto *Claudel Thomiste?* And she wrote her term paper on it, an essay so far above the average that Roger could not help cultivating the girl. Like himself, she hardly fitted into what the university had become, a mindless recitation of technical knowledge or the mad attacks on the culture a university was supposed to transmit. Francie became one of the little group of coeds known somewhat derisively as the Ladies of Knight. Paul's cousin Vivian was another.

With all this as prelude, Roger was not surprised when Francie called to say that she was on campus and could she come see him.

9 AS AN INSTITUTION ADVANCES from humble beginnings to ever greater distinction and prestige, there are casualties of its progress. Teachers hired in a time of more modest expectations find themselves surrounded by younger and more ambitious colleagues, publications and involvement in professional societies become an expected thing, and many of the old guard, their habits formed in a different atmosphere, find it impossible to conform. So it is that the final decades of a professorial career can be accompanied by bitterness and resentment of the changes that have rendered one all but obsolete. A dinosaur in the modern world. At the university club a table was claimed by those who called themselves and were called by others, with somewhat different emphasis, the Old Bastards. Summer did not alter their habit of meeting at least twice a week for lunch and grousing about the decay and dissolution of the university. Vexation at the new had become a mark of virtue among them and it was mandatory to lament any change, particularly those heralded by the administration.

"A National Catholic Research University," Bruno Basset

said, emphasizing each word of the loathsome phrase now etched in signs at the various entrances to the campus.

"What is a national Catholic?" Potsdam asked. "It is contradictory. A universal specialist."

Angoscia, who had lived out his active life as a member of what was called the General Program of Liberal Studies, bristled. "A generalist must be an individual."

" 'I was that narrowest of specialists, the well-rounded man,' " Armitage Shanks murmured.

"Who said that?"

"Nick Carraway."

"Never heard of him."

"He is the narrator of *The Great Gatsby*."

Debbie the hostess came by to refill coffee cups and was shamelessly flirted with by the impotent denizens of the Old Bastards table. She flounced away, not unflattered by their attention. It was said in whispers that she had suggested that the senior employees of the club call themselves the Old Bitches.

"Someone fell dead on the golf course this morning," Basset said.

"Which golf course?"

Grumbling began. The exercise of eminent domain over the back nine of the Burke golf course was the sort of thing the Old Bastards could make a meal of. Only Shanks among them had ever golfed, but they were prepared to regard the confiscation of that land as a personal assault on them all.

"The spring before construction began," Shanks said, beginning an oft-told tale, "during midyear break when all is

48

deserted, even the Morris Inn, the campus a wasteland, I parked behind the inn, threw my clubs over the fence, clambered over after them, and played holes thirteen through eighteen three times. I pride myself on being the last one to play those holes."

"They should put up a plaque," Bruno muttered.

"You have to be a golfer to understand."

"That explains it."

"Who died on the golf course?"

"Mortimer Sadler."

"Sadler?"

"That's right. He gave the money for the new dorm named after him."

The next ten minutes were devoted to lamentation on the constant campus construction, the inelegance of the architecture, the filling of every available space with some new monstrosity.

"The one genuine improvement is the benches."

"The benches are a blessing." Along every campus walk now, at intervals of perhaps twenty-five yards, there was a bench on which tired bones could be rested.

"Speaking of plaques . . ."

Groans. On each bench was a plaque commemorating the donor or the one whom the donor wished the bench to commemorate.

"Have you ever been to Paris?" Bruno asked.

The others stared at him in silence.

"Or Rome. Or Rapallo, for that matter. One will find in Rapallo plaques commemorating Ezra Pound's long stay there, the fact that Nietzsche wrote part of *Thus Spake Zarathustra* there, and that it was also in that lovely town that Sibelius composed a movement of one of his symphonies."

"Are they on benches?"

"On the walls of buildings."

"Oh, well . . ."

"The principle is the same."

But Bruno's analogy was summarily rejected and he was ignored.

"I had a Sadler in class," Bruno said. "But that was years ago."

"He was in the class of 1977."

"Perhaps he was the one. He died?"

"They found him on the sixth green, dead as a doornail."

"What is the meaning of that phrase?"

Another diversion. Meanwhile, Bruno sat in awed wonder at the thought that a student of his had preceded him in death, in the obituary phrase. A small triumphant smile formed on his chapped lips that he found impossible to suppress.

DENNIS GRANTLEY WALKED SLOW-
ly up the sloping path to the starter's
building on the first tee of the Burke golf course. The late
afternoon sun shone at a painful slant, but it was not the sun
that brought the squint to Max's eyes; they squinted in all seasons and at all times of day.

"You heard about it?" Max asked.

" 'It'?" Grantley eased himself onto a bench and shielded
his eyes from the setting sun.

"The big excitement here this morning."

Grantley had heard little else all day—in the Huddle
where he had his breakfast, in the Warren clubhouse where he
had his lunch, and in the maintenance shed from which he
had just come. There old Swannie had pointed out just where
the golf cart used by Mortimer Sadler had been parked until it
was taken away in a police truck.

"They put a big sign on the windshield. 'Don't touch.' Who
would want to touch the damned thing?"

The maintenance shed smelled of oil and grease and the
sick, sweet smell of the grass that was wedged in the blades of
the mowers and in the treads of their tires. Swannie had a little office in a corner, the door of which was always open lest

he miss anything in the shed. Windows gave him a view of the Rockne across the road and the starter's building to the right.

"Fingerprints," Grantley suggested.

Swannie looked at his grease-stained hands. He still went out on a mower from time to time to keep his hand in, but by and large he let the boys hired for the summer keep the fairways and greens trim. But he himself personally made sure that all the course machinery was in order. He was presiding over the demise of Burke and had assumed an appropriately melancholy air. He had come to work here as a young man, in the glory days of the course. Who would have thought then that its days were numbered, that a time would come when the back nine would disappear and a row of pompous buildings stand where greens and traps and fairways once had been? It was the end of an era.

Of course Grantley had seen the cart and the sign coming from the Huddle, where he first heard of the death on the golf course. Shortly after he arrived, the police came to take the cart away and Grantley had wandered over to the Rockne, where he had a smoke seated at the one table left in the golf shop. Once groups of faculty and administrators had frequented the tables in the shop, whiling away the time before or after a round. Grantley had been an assistant golf coach and had spent much of the day in the shop year-round. When he first arrived on campus, there had been a physical education department and he had faculty status, but when the department was dissolved and he was retained as assistant golf coach his status had become equivocal. Freshmen still took a credit in physical education and golf lessons were one

52

of the options, so Grantley had been kept occupied, but he was no longer on the staff that coached the golf team, which in recent years had dramatically grown in number. Thus he wandered ghostlike around the campus, haunting it with memories of other times.

As he had with Swannie, he let Max give him the news as if he had not heard it.

"A funny thing, Dennis. He was the Sadler that they named one of the halls over on twelve and thirteen after."

"What's funny about that?"

"He has a lot of guts playing on the course he helped ruin."

Grantley said nothing. The complaints and grievances of others were as nothing to his own, but by and large he preferred to nurse his resentment in silence. His life had been a slow descent from his first position at Notre Dame, each change dropping him lower on the scale until he had achieved a kind of anonymity as he wandered about the campus. He could sit in the lunchroom at Warren without being recognized, as if he were a stranger. From time to time a middle-aged player, come in for a beer between nines, would glance at him quizzically, but he was seldom approached. He could count the times he had been asked, "Say, didn't you give golf lessons once?" The last time he had told the questioner he was mistaken. What the hell good could such uncertain recognition do to offset the injustice that had been done him?

Yes, injustice. Sundays in Sacred Heart, at an early Mass—the earlier the better—he often heard sermons on peace and justice, but the priest never made an application of those lofty principles to the university's own practices. The villains were always out there in the world, their misdeeds having to be undone or balanced by the efforts of those in the pews. Notre Dame was now the largest employer in town and people eagerly sought jobs on campus for less pay than they could get elsewhere, if there was an elsewhere available to them. If they were exploited it was willingly, and that, Grantley admitted, had been the case with himself. At first. He would have paid to be on the faculty at Notre Dame in those days. But the declining line of his local status had brought a resentment he hardly dared to formulate in his mind, let alone declare openly. The truth was, he was torn between an undiminished, almost holy love for the university and rage at its practices. His resolution of this dilemma was to blame the administration and exempt Notre Dame itself.

"He was just being generous," he said to Max, exonerating Sadler in words. But of course his thoughts about the man made Max's seem benevolent.

"They say he was poisoned."

"Wasn't he playing alone?"

"How the hell would I know? He took a cart and went out before I got here."

When Swannie mentioned poison, Grantley had kidded him about the gunk he put on the greens and fairways. Before the sprinkling system had been put in, the fairways were hard to keep green. By August they had become khaki colored and slippery, so a duffer's scudded ball could end up two hundred yards out on the fairway. Burke had been one of the first beneficiaries of the university's affluence. A sprinkler system was installed, the ground crew increased in number, all kinds of chemical treatments applied to fairways and greens.

"He probably chewed on a blade of grass and keeled over."

"You think I put poison on the greens?"

"Only the fairways."

"Bah."

Now Grantley sat on the bench, listening to Max grouse. Sometimes he thought there was a chorus of the disenchanted, oldsters whose time at Notre Dame had been a long decline. That was life, one might think, generation supplanted by generation, those about to go into the dark lamenting the lack of light, cursing the young who either ignored or disdained them. His own grievances were made sotto voce, spoken only to himself in the privacy of his room on the second floor of the Firehouse, a monkish cell in which he lived out the twilight of his life.

He had been in the bar of the Morris Inn when the irregulars of the class of 1977 arrived to register, alerted to their coming by Agnes, a waitress in the restaurant with designs on Grantley that he did not wholly discourage. The thought of marriage was as foreign to him as a vocation to the Carthusians, but it was pleasant to be the object of feminine attention. Agnes had been a divorcée, and was now a widow, a veteran of the dining room, carrying a few extra pounds that were pleasantly distributed. Her ample bosom was the promise of an almost maternal comforting, though Grantley had never availed himself of its promise. His conscience had been formed as a boy and sins of the flesh were the paradigm of wrongdoing, the subject of his first terrified adolescent whispering through the grille of the confessional. His relationship with Agnes was accordingly platonic but with the constant suggestion of a more that never got realized. He thought of her as his personal occasion of sin.

"Who's registered?"

"Who? There must be fifty or more."

"Can you get me the roster?"

She could and did, a computer printout of reservations. The name of Mortimer Sadler lifted from the page, the sum of all his discontents. In the bar, he had watched them enter in twos and threes and more, huddle at the bar, take tables. Sadler was the noisiest, of course, and Grantley, brooding over his drink in an ill-lit corner, watched the man with malevolent eyes. If there was a symbol of his decline in status on campus it was Mortimer Sadler, as if he singlehandedly was responsible for the desecration of Burke. The man's voice was full of the pride of life, a voice without doubts, a menace. Grantley sat and thought confessable thoughts about the man.

11 FRANCIE HAD BEEN ASKED TO the Knight apartment for dinner, meaning supper, with five-thirty given as the time of her arrival, and decided to ignore the vague plan to dine with her mother.

"That will give us a chance for some conversation before Phil gets here," Roger had said.

Francie was thrilled by this sign of election. That she was able to take his class was in itself an enormous plus, but to be regarded as a favored student was bliss indeed. At five-thirty on the dot she rang the bell.

A minute passed before Roger Knight, his face aglow from his efforts in the kitchen, swathed in an enormous apron that reached from his chest to his ankles—enough material to make a tent, as he said—opened the door, greeted her, and bowed her into the room. Their greeting was a formal handshake. No hugging and backslapping from Roger Knight. But there was little doubt about the delight with which he greeted her.

"How is your summer going?"

Suddenly she felt ashamed of the indolence that had marked her time at home. Sleeping late, catching up with old friends, golfing. She had gone home with a list of the books she intended to read, but so far she had not even begun.

"Oh, fine. What have you been doing?"

And he was off and running, telling her what he was reading, the exchanges with his far-flung e-mail pals, comments on changes in the university, the latest squabbles at the highest levels, a veritable flow of interests—"trivia and quadrivia"—that made Francie's life seem impossibly monochrome. But for the moment it was enough to bask in the participated glow of Roger Knight's interests. Had she ever met anyone she would more like to be like than Roger Knight? Of course this seemed an odd ambition. She could not become a bachelor weighing nearly three hundred pounds who held an endowed chair at Notre Dame. But it was not the possibility of exact imitation that drew her to Roger Knight. He exuded the realization that there was a way to spend one's life that was infinitely exciting and totally unlike the lives most people led, including, so far as she could see, most other members of the faculty. In vain had she tried to convey her enthusiasm for Roger Knight to Paul.

"The fat guy?"

"Is that all you can say about him?"

"I couldn't get into his class. I tried."

"Did you ask him?"

But she could not believe that Roger Knight could have even remotely seen in Paul the possibilities he had seen in her. Paul was perfectly content to while away his summer in campus sports camps. But even as she thought this lofty condemnation she remembered the way she had been spending her own summer. Who was she to cast the first stone? So she and Paul had talked about her golf game that morning, playing with her mother in the alumni tournament. She was with him when news of his uncle's death arrived. He looked blankly at Francie. She in turn looked blankly at him. For a terrible moment she wondered if he had understood the awful news. Neither of them had any experience with such an event. Nor, of course, had Francie even known the uncle who had been found dead on the old course.

"What was he doing there, Paul? He was due to play on Warren."

"Don't ask me. This is my SOB uncle."

As soon as he said it he seemed to regret it. Francie went with him to the Morris Inn, where the police were talking to old friends of Mortimer Sadler. It was then that they learned that his death was not considered to be accidental. Mortimer Sadler had died of poisoning.

"Food poisoning?"

Lieutenant Stewart looked at Paul and shook his head. When Paul introduced her to the detective, he perked up.

"O'Kelly? There is a Mrs. O'Kelly registered here."

"So am I. She's my mother."

"And you came with her to her class reunion?"

"Oh, this doesn't really count. She came in order to . . ." Francie fell silent. How to explain her mother's pique that Mortimer Sadler had the gall to arrange an all-male get-together and call it a class reunion? Francie felt none of her mother's competitive feminism. Going to St. Mary's rather than Notre Dame had been a way of avoiding the duplication of her mother's determination to rival any and every male achievement. Her mother's feminist zeal had led to an estrangement

59

from Francie's father, the marriage forever teetering on the brink of collapse, until now there was a trial separation that Francie prayed would end in reunion. In the locker room of the Minikahda Club in Minneapolis, Mortimer had confronted Jack O'Kelly, drunkenly commenting on his unseemly conduct for a Notre Dame alumnus. And he had referred to Maureen as Superwoman. O'Kelly, normally the mildest of men, obliged with a blow that sent Sadler sprawling. Small wonder that Francie had not told her mother that she was seeing Paul Sadler. It would have seemed like an ideological statement rather than a real attraction.

"She wanted a partner for golf."

Stewart found that more interesting than it was and Paul told him Francie's handicap.

"Is that good?"

"It's half mine."

Why did she think the detective already knew a low handicap when he heard one? It was the first intimation she had that the man thought her mother's long-standing quarrel with Mortimer Sadler might have some connection with Sadler's death.

"I'm told your mother is quite a gardener."

"Who told you that?"

"Your mother."

"She's bragging."

But not much. The O'Kelly yard and flower beds had been featured in a recent garden walk in Minneapolis. Her mother's habit of drawing attention to her own accomplishments made it unsurprising that she had mentioned the garden walk and whose flowers had drawn such praise.

"A woman has a right to brag of her gardening."

Oh, if her mother had heard that remark!

"She also mentioned her golf handicap."

"She seems to have told you everything."

"I hope so."

"Has the family been notified?" Paul asked.

"His widow is on her way."

"Widow. I better call some of my cousins."

"Vivian," Francie suggested.

"Of course."

The task seemed a reason for Francie to not mention her invitation to dine with the Knight brothers. Paul got busy with his cell phone and Francie went to her room, where her mother came humming from the shower.

"I've been talking with the police," Francie said.

"Detective Stewart?"

"Yes."

"Dreadful man. Condescending. He asked if I played from the ladies' tee."

"Well, you do."

"It's the way he asked."

Since high school, Francie had learned what it must be like for twins, everyone telling her how much like her mother she looked. She knew her mother was beautiful, but it was not the kind of beauty Francie preferred, perhaps because of the constant comparison.

"Have you showered?"

"That's why I'm here."

"Where have you been?"

"I ran into someone I met in class."

"The conditions at Warren are barbaric. It's little more than a shrine to the golf team. The men's team, of course."

"Is there a women's team?"

Her mother thought about it. "There better be."

"Isn't it awful about Mr. Sadler?"

Her mother had to think about that, too. "Yes, of course."

When Francie came from the shower, her mother was lying on the bed, in her robe. "I think I'll take a little nap. Where would you like to eat?"

"Would you mind if I ate with some friends?"

"What friends?"

"Professor Knight asked me over."

"Who is he?"

"Mother, I have told you all about him."

"The fat man?"

"You sound like Paul."

"Who's Paul?"

"The boy I ran into."

"Is he going, too?"

"No."

"I hope I'm not expected."

"Mother, you wouldn't enjoy it at all."

Her mother was already on the phone, saying she would call some old classmates who had settled in South Bend.

Francie had slipped away to the Knight apartment without running into Paul.

When Roger's brother, Phil, arrived at the Knight apartment he had Detective Stewart with him. For an awful moment Francie feared that he would start quizzing her about her mother again, but Roger bustled them right into the meal, dishing spaghetti from a huge bowl into which he poured some hot water before mixing it up. The salad bowl was almost as large as the pasta bowl and there were heaps of garlic bread and a huge carafe of red wine, although Roger drank ice water with his meal. And talked. The other two men just listened and busied themselves with their food. As soon as they were done, they adjourned to the television for a ball game and Francie had Roger all to herself.

"I'll help with the dishes."

"Wonderful. Phil is little help."

It was not a complaint. Francie marveled at how well the brothers got along. During dinner, she had been told of the loss of their parents when Roger was in his early teens and the way Phil had assumed the role of father to prevent their being separated. Phil dismissed all that, preferring to talk about how Roger had been considered retarded through much of school until someone had finally recognized that he was a genius.

"Nonsense!" Roger said.

"Tell her your score."

"I will not. Such tests are idiotic. They cause much more harm than anything else."

"It certainly ruined your life."

"I never said that."

How had it been to be a prodigy at Princeton and a Ph.D. at an age when most boys were finishing high school? Unable to find academic employment, Roger had actually joined the navy.

"What did you do in the navy?"

"Well, I passed the swimming test."

"By floating the length of the pool," Phil said, but his laughter was affectionate. Francie had come to like him, too, but tonight she was glad he had taken Jimmy Stewart off to watch television. After they finished the dishes, Francie had another glass of wine at the kitchen table and Roger sat across from her and talked. It might have been one of his seminars.

"He questioned me about the death on the golf course," Francie whispered.

"Jimmy Stewart? Whatever for?"

"I was with the nephew of the man who was killed."

"One should speak well of the dead so I shall be silent."

"Did you know him?"

"No. But I have heard more about him than I wished to know."

"His nephew is nice."

"Ah."

She let it go. Let him think what he liked. It was oddly pleasant to imagine that he might be jealous, but that was so ridiculous Francie laughed.

12 CAL SWITHINS HAD BEEN RE-
lieved when Jimmy Stewart did not
turn in at the campus entrance but continued on to the
Morris Inn. He had been practicing what he would say
to the guard at the gate. Perhaps, "Press," said casu-
ally while pretending to look around as he avoided the
guard's eyes. But now there was no need to run the risk
of the refusal this ruse might have earned. Anyone
could park in the Morris Inn parking lot, the assumption being that they were guests or had come to dine in
the restaurant. Thus it was that he had hung about in
the lobby, unobserved, while Stewart and Knight spoke
to a succession of the dead man's friends. But it was in
the men's room downstairs that he heard the mention of
poison. His pulse quickened. Now he was certain he
was on to something while Raskow lolled about in the
press room at police headquarters.

When he emerged into the lobby, he ran into Phil Knight.

"Get what you were looking for?"

"Where is the Alumni Center?"

Phil Knight came outside with him and pointed him up
Notre Dame Avenue. Swithins had little choice but to set off.

When he got to his car he looked back. Knight was nowhere in evidence, so Swithins headed west along a campus walk in the direction of what remained of the old golf course.

When he came to the road that ran along the golf course fence, he continued toward Rockne Memorial. There was an old guy on the practice putting green and Swithins stopped to watch him. Hunched over his ball, the man seemed aware of his presence. He turned and glared at Swithins.

"What can I do for you?"

"Teach me how to golf, I'll bet."

Unexpectedly, the man smiled. "What class were you in?"

"Nineteen eighty-two." This was the year Swithins had graduated from high school in Syracuse.

"I'm not good at names."

"Swithins. Cal Swithins."

"I'm Dennis Grantley, of course." He held out his hand.

"Of course."

"What brings you back?"

For answer, Swithins opened his arms and looked around. Grantley nodded as if he understood.

"This the first time you've seen what they've done to this golf course?"

"When did it happen?"

Grantley led him to a bench and sat down with a grunt. He had used his putter as a cane and now began hitting his right shoe with the club head. "It's a sad story."

But one he seemed happy enough to tell. Swithins listened patiently to this tale of woe. Finally, Grantley was done.

"Terrible what happened to Mortimer Sadler."

"Did you know him?"

Swithins shrugged.

"You said '82. He was before your time."

"The name is familiar."

"I'll tell you why. See that ugly building over there? That is the Mortimer Sadler Residence Hall."

"He must have done well."

"A helluva lot of difference it makes now. What do you do?"

"I write. I'm a reporter." He looked thoughtful. "I would like to write up what you've told me about the golf course."

"Who would print it?"

"*The Notre Dame Magazine?*"

"Ha."

"I heard that Sadler was poisoned."

"Where did you hear that?"

"At the Morris Inn."

"So that's where you're staying. You ought to write up Sadler's death."

"That is a very good idea. Did you know him well?"

"I suppose not much better than I knew you. But he came back often. And, of course, he donated that building. But you will probably want to concentrate on what happened this morning."

Swithins got out a notebook and brought the tip of his pencil to his tongue. Over the next hour, he scribbled down everything Grantley told him and then they went across the road to the maintenance shed, where a man named Swannie added his two cents. Grantley left him there in Swannie's office, but nothing Swithins heard added much to what he already had. By now he was anxious to get downtown.

Half an hour later, he was in the city room. The sight of it brought an unexpected lump to his throat. Raskow was not there but Mendax, the city editor, was in his glassed-in office, mixing something milky in a glass. He looked out at Swithins and his expression was not welcoming. Swithins opened the door and went in.

"Shut that damned door."

Swithins shut the damned door. "I want your go-ahead on a story."

"You were fired."

"Mistakes are made."

"What was yours?"

"That isn't what I meant. Look, Lyman, I'm on to something big. There has been a murder on the Notre Dame campus—"

But Mendax held up his hand. "Stop right there. You ought to know that this paper is not going to put the university in a bad light."

"The university didn't murder him."

"Stop using that word."

"It's the only word that fits."

"Maybe it is, maybe it isn't. Raskow has already written a story on Sadler's falling dead on the golf course."

"Raskow hasn't been on campus. I have. I've interviewed people, I have all the facts."

But Mendax just kept shaking his head. "Stick with obits, Swithins."

So he knew about that. But Mendax had become the editorial equivalent of a stone wall. Swithins felt beaten.

"I'll write the death notice," he said.

"Good. But don't use incendiary language."

Swithins went into the city room and sat at a computer. He felt like crying. But by God, this was his big chance. He would write this story if he had to place it in *The Shopper*. He got up and stormed out of the city room. No one noticed him leave.

13 IN HIS ROOM AT HOLY CROSS House, Father Carmody put down his breviary and asked Dennis Grantley if he would like something.

"Like what?"

"A beer?"

"If that is the best you can do."

Thus induced, Father Carmody got out a bottle of Powers and poured a niggardly ounce for his less-than-welcome guest.

"So you have been wandering about the world like the devil in Job."

Grantley sipped his whiskey and ignored the remark. Once Carmody had been a golfer, but he had quit the game when he despaired of eventually shooting his age. Once on the course, nothing was more pleasant, but it became increasingly difficult to waste from three to five hours or more establishing the fact that his game was not what it had been. Grantley was an old friend, of sorts, a man who had been about the campus almost as long as the old priest, but he was an uncomfortable reminder of the passage of time. Father Carmody had moved to Holy Cross House from Corby, the clerical residence on campus, without complaint, refusing to see it for what it was, the last station on the journey of life. Others in the house were in various stages of their final illness. Once a week there was a melancholy row of wheelchairs filled with those awaiting a haircut, once-mighty figures reduced by strokes or worse to drooling oldsters submissive to whatever they were wheeled to endure.

Carmody himself remained hale and hearty. He might have stayed on campus, but even the seniors there had seemed young whelps to him, and he preferred the autonomy of Holy Cross. He could get around by golf cart or drive when he chose to leave the campus. His room here was much as his room had been wherever he had lived on campus, and he had dwelt in a succession of buildings—first in the Main Building, when residence there was not unusual, then moving on to a hall where he had been rector before he would have been ignominiously removed from under the Golden Dome in the Main Building. In his mind's eye, his present quarters were simply his present quarters; such intimations of mortality as came to him were applicable to others rather than himself. His grandfather had lived to a hundred and both his parents were gaga in their nineties when God called them to Himself. His own mind was clear, his energy somewhat diminished but, with judicious napping, adequate, his physical examinations productive of unwelcome praise from physicians, as if his health were some accomplishment, a product of his will. Father Carmody recognized a grace when he received one.

The most difficult task of all is growing old. This was a truth he had come to see as much in the breach as in the observance. Grantley had not grown old gracefully. He repined. He groused. He resented. And he lapped up Powers as if it were water. Carmody replenished his glass, his own scarcely touched. Temperance was an easy virtue.

"You heard about Sadler?"

"Which one?"

"Mortimer. They found him dead on the sixth green of Burke this morning."

Of course Carmody had heard it all, but there was a mordant pleasure in allowing Grantley to tell the story as if it were news.

"Poison," Grantley said, smacking his lips. "The poor wretch must have taken his own life."

"Never presume that, Dennis. The police do not."

"How do you know?"

Father Carmody made an impatient wave of his hand. "The question is, who would have wanted to kill the man?"

"I could make a list."

"Come now."

"You remember him as an undergraduate, I am sure. In the early seventies. Mad as a hornet about the fact that women had been admitted to Notre Dame."

"That was long ago."

"Barley is my favorite suspect."

"Barley!"

"They shared a quad in St. Edward's."

"Two in a quad?"

"Oh, there were four of them. But Barley had the strongest motive."

"What an odd fellow you are, Grantley."

"He is here for the reunion Sadler defiantly initiated as a thumb in the eye of the alumni association. They were to be a foursome at Warren, the four old roommates. They whooped it up in the Morris Inn last night and early this morning Sadler crept out on Burke for some practice holes. That is why he was found there."

"He was playing alone?"

"What killed him was in his water bottle."

Philip Knight had already reported this to Carmody by telephone. "What does belladonna suggest to you, Father?" he'd asked.

"I am a celibate."

"She is a poison."

"What a chauvinist you are."

"Roger tells me that chauvinist has something to do with baldness. My hair is still thick."

"You mean that Mortimer Sadler was poisoned?"

"That was the first result of the police investigation."

This was dire news. High on Father Carmody's list of priorities was that only good should be spoken of Notre Dame, and if evil occurred it was to be discreetly muffled if not entirely silenced.

"Have the media been told?"

"It's hardly a secret."

The media! The plural of *medium*, a medium being one who conducted séances and invoked the powers of evil to wreak havoc in the world. Only such a profession would have accepted such a designation. Father Carmody, of course, exempted the alumni who had done well in journalism.

"What are you going to do?" Grantley asked now, studying his empty glass. Father Carmody had capped the Powers after pouring Grantley a second tot and was indisposed to open it anew.

"What do you mean?"

"We can't have a scandal."

Grantley's remark reminded him of his feeling of impotence when Phil Knight had passed on the news. He had asked Roger Knight's brother to represent the university in the matter, the better to prevent public attention. But it would have been delinquent of the local constabulary to treat a murder on campus as if it were a secret.

"This would have been unthinkable once," Grantley said.

Carmody said nothing. A local woman had compiled an unpublished manuscript on the strange and unsolved deaths on the Notre Dame campus. Any acreage in the world chosen at random might deliver up similar mysteries. Was Grantley really unaware of the precedents? More likely his remark was simply another instance of his resolve to treat the present as a betrayal of the past.

"The more quickly it is solved the better."

"The murderer found?"

"I thought you suspected suicide."

"It was my first thought. But that is so horrible to contemplate."

Grantley's tone indicated that he would have welcomed an exchange on the inscrutable ways of Providence, the folly of men, the mercy of God, and allied subjects. The fact was that the man annoyed Father Carmody, all the more because of his manifest assumption that they were in the same boat. Grantley considered his own years at Notre Dame to be a record of unjust treatment and feeble loyalty to one who had given his life to the university. He had a case of sorts, but what was the point of making it again and again? If it came from another it might elicit more sympathy, but no one can plead his own case without weakening it. Besides, Carmody did not see his own life as one of failure. There are seasons in human life and he accepted the one in which he now found himself.

"You must pray for him, Dennis."

"That is difficult. I knew him."

"All the more meritorious."

Grantley held his glass to the light as if to verify its emptiness. Carmody did not take the hint. He stood.

"You better get to your bed, Dennis."

"It isn't nine o'clock."

"That is the witching hour here."

"I don't know how you can stand this place."

"There were no empty rooms in the firehouse."

That was mean, and in repayment Father Carmody accompanied Grantley to the front entrance and through the sliding doors into the summer night.

"Don't tell me you walked."

"They make me park my car off campus now."

"You should get a bicycle."

Another mean remark. Grantley's artifical knees would have made biking painful. Father Carmody patted his visitor on the back and sent him shuffling into the night. Back in his room he offered up a prayer in reparation for his lack of sympathy with Dennis Grantley. And for the repose of the soul of Mortimer Sadler.

14 THE ARCHIVES OF THE UNIVERsity of Notre Dame are located on the sixth floor of the Hesburgh Library. When the library was opened in 1963 it was vaguely called the Memorial Library, and donors of various degrees and dimensions were commemorated on plaques throughout the building. The first archivist, Father McEvoy, a distinguished if curmudgeonly historian, died at his post and was found one Monday morning at his desk. Eventually, the name of the library was changed to honor Father Theodore M. Hesburgh, the legendary president of the university who had retired, after decades in office, into an aerie on the thirteenth floor along with his long-time associate, Edmund Joyce, ostensibly to enjoy such years of leisure as might be left them. In any event, Hesburgh's career had accelerated in his supposed retirement, and while he studiously attempted to keep in the background his successors were faced with the formidably eclipsing fact of his presence.

As they awaited a building commensurate with their holdings, the archives continued to operate in their original quarters in the library, since expanded by various timorous forays into abutting territory, until almost the entire sixth floor was at the disposal of the archives. It was not enough. The denizens and votaries of the archives lived in the expectation that the day would come when quarters proportionate to the extent and value of its holdings would be provided. Among them was Greg Whelan.

Like many who are employed in university libraries, Whelan's career had been a varied one. He had a Ph.D. in classics but because of a debilitating stammer, it had proved useless to him so far as employment went. He then acquired an LL.B. in the quixotic hope that preparing himself for a forensic career would somehow loosen his tongue and turn him overnight into a Demosthenes of the courtroom. It had not. In the end he got a degree in library science, was hired by the Notre Dame archives, and ever since had enjoyed the happiest days of his life. Not least among the reasons for this was his friendship with Roger Knight.

Doubtless a hundred useless theories could be devised to account for the fact that with Roger, Greg Whelan's stammer ceased and the two unusual individuals conversed with an ease and range that would have been the marvel of any witnesses, if witnesses would not have rendered Greg Whelan mute. A chance remark of Roger's had unleashed him on such holdings of the archives as might cast light on the demise of Mortimer Sadler.

For much of the university's history a publication called *The Scholastic* had been the campus journal of record. Among its contributors had been numbered faculty of repute as well as gifted students. Through many permutations from the nineteenth into the twentieth century it had recorded and chronicled the doings of the legendary South Bend campus. In the turbulent sixties of the twentieth century—harbinger of many other changes to come, some representing progress, others mere change—a campus publication had been founded to contest the hegemony of *The Scholastic*. A product of antinomian times, inspired by the tiresome liberalism of the day, it had been rapidly transformed from an underground publication, a kind of samizdat of dissent, into the accepted daily newspaper of the university. (*The Scholastic*, bereft of its former greatness, continued as a badly printed weekly whose ineffectual sensationalism did not offset the fact that it, was merely a relic of a forgotten past.)

The Observer, still in the first feisty days of its antiestablishmentarianism, had provided a platform for the crusade that Mortimer Sadler, hardly the most effective pen on campus, launched against the novelty of coeducation at Notre Dame. The day after Sadler's death Greg Whelan searched out and photocopied the lengthy series of diatribes Mortimer Sadler had penned. Letters of protest and contention filled the paper whenever he appeared. His was not a position universally accepted. At the outset, the male population of Notre Dame had apparently thought that coeducation was a device meant to provide each of them with a suitable object of affection. But the manner of accepting women students, concentrating exclusively on talent and test scores, insured that Mortimer Sadler's campaign had adherents as well as dissenters. At that time, the female population of the student body was outnumbered by males in a massive manner. For all that, some males and those females who sought to counter the Sadler campaign were eloquent, however insignificant their actual numbers. Among them was Maureen Jensen, destined to be the valedictorian of the class of 1977.

Her pithy and deadly responses to Sadler provided a literate and delightful counterpoint to his campaign, and Greg Whelan dutifully photocopied them all. The results, abstracted from their provenance, suggested a pointed and lively debate on an issue that only a chauvinist could deny Maureen had won.

"Whatever became of her?" Roger asked.

"She married an internist named O'Kelly."

"O'Kelly?"

"Yes," Greg said, correctly reading Roger's reaction. "The very woman who is registered at the Morris Inn. If Sadler was her nemesis, she was his Waterloo."

"To mix a metaphor."

"A metaphor is already a mixture."

"Touché. Are these all the articles?" Roger ruffled the bundle of sheets Greg had given him.

"All."

"There are other items in which the two figure, but unrelated to this controversy."

"Such as?"

Greg combed his beard with his fingers. "She seems to have won every academic prize offered, even a poetry prize."

"Really?"

"A villanelle called 'Why a Good Man Is Hard to Find.' "

"What is the answer?"

"You have to lose him first."

"She does sound the feminine counterpart of the youthful Mortimer Sadler."

"And she won the Midland Naturalist prize for breeding a new species of tulip."

"A veritable Renaissance woman. I should like to meet her."

"Perhaps she has mellowed with age."

"She certainly has a lovely daughter."

"Indeed."

"You know her?"

"Roger, I met her at your semester-end party."

"Of course."

Roger had given the party for his students of both the fall and spring semesters, renting a large room at the university club for the purpose. Of course he had invited Greg as well, but in such a crowd the archivist had been rendered mute. For all that, he seemed to have enjoyed it. Roger now remembered that he had deputized Francie to entertain Greg and she had been at his side most of the evening, chattering pleasantly and relieving him of the need to stutter.

"She visited the archives the following week. I had told her how prominent a student her mother was."

"So you did talk to her?"

"Yes." Greg was half indignant, as if he forgot he had a speech impediment.

"So you had already dug up half this material months ago?"

"Oh, she wasn't interested in her mother's accomplishments. She asked to see anything I had on her father."

"Jack O'Kelly? So he was a student here as well."

"Before his future wife arrived on campus. He was in the class of 1970."

"And did you find anything?"

"Dozens of poems. Mostly sonnets. They were all written to someone named Laura."

"Petrarchan sonnets?"

Greg smiled. "They were either translations or close imitations. I don't think his daughter believed me. She wanted me to identify Laura."

"Easily enough done."

"Not when she is thought to be a student."

"But that would have been before coeducation."

"I checked all the Lauras at St. Mary's during the years O'Kelly was a student at Notre Dame and gave them to Francie."

"To what end?"

Roger did not approve of Greg encouraging Francie in her misunderstanding. It seemed obvious that her father had taken over the poetry and the dedicatee of Petrarch's sonnets.

"Oh, she was satisfied enough. There was a Minneapolis Laura Kennedy who is a longtime friend of the family. She never married, and Francie clearly thought she had been heartbroken when O'Kelly's interest waned and condemned her to a single life."

"You must ask her if she has found anything to verify this romantic theory."

"I was hoping you would, Roger."

15 "WHAT WERE YOU AND MORT AR-
guing about the other night?" Crown
asked Toolin.

"Last night?"

"After we left. I was almost ready for bed when I realized I
had not taken my drink with me when I left Mort's suite, for a
nightcap. So I tiptoed back there in my pajamas and was
about to knock when I heard the two of you going at it."

"It was nothing serious."

"It sounded serious."

"We were both half smashed. We both said things we
wouldn't have said otherwise."

"About Maureen?"

"You really had your ear pressed to the door, didn't you?"

"It wasn't necessary. Anyway, I decided it was none of my
business and went to bed. I needed another drink like I
needed a hole in the head."

Ever since the discovery of Mort's body, Toolin had been
thinking of the fact that the last time he had seen his old
roommate they had quarreled. Toolin had not liked the way
Sadler spoke of the O'Kelly marriage. Dr. O'Kelly meant nothing to Toolin—he had graduated before they had arrived on

campus—but Toolin's sense of gallantry had been sharpened by alcohol and he had risen to the lady's defense.

"The fact is, Mort, you loved her. I remember how you used to follow her around. It's because she gave you the bum's rush that all the other stuff followed."

"What other stuff?"

"Your big campaign to return Notre Dame to an all-male student body. It was just sour grapes, Mort, and it's ridiculous to keep it up. You're a happily married man, she's a happily married woman . . ."

"There, my dear fellow, I beg to differ with you." Sadler was apt to slip into his imitation of one of their old professors, Tom Stritch, when he got drunk. But he waggled his brows in an un-Stritchian way.

"What do you mean?"

"Trouble in paradise, my good man. They are separated. But she is as much sinned against as sinning. The good doctor has renewed a passion of his student days, a friend of my older sister, Laura Kennedy."

"My God, he must be nearly sixty."

"So what? Haven't you heard of Viagra?"

"It's where we went on our honeymoon."

"Not Niagra. In any case, the lady is a tramp as well as trampled on."

"What lady?"

"Who are we talking about?"

"Laura somebody."

"No, no. Maureen O'Kelly."

"It is wrong to say such things of her."

84

It was not so much that they were arguing as that they both had spoken at the top of their voices, enunciating carefully and with thick tongues. Toolin had caught Mort in the face with a sofa cushion on his way out, pulling the door shut on his lucky shot. How sobering to realize that was the last time he was to see Mort alive. That melancholy realization kept the conversation heavy on his mind during the next twenty-four hours. But the exchange took on a different aspect when Stewart and Philip Knight talked to him the second time.

"What were you fighting with Sadler about the night before he died?"

Crown must have passed this on, but why? He must know that the police were professionally suspicious. Good God, they talked to him as if he himself had something to do with the death of Mort. Toolin tried to dismiss it as nothing but soon, as he had with Crown, he told them what he and Mort had been talking about after the others left the suite.

ARMITAGE SHANKS TOOK AN INI-
tial sip of his executive martini, so
called because it was served in a small carafe that yielded a
glass and a half—or two, if one dallied and permitted the ice
to melt. Across from him at the Old Bastards table in the university club, Ambrose Dulcedo followed Shanks's testing of
his drink with avid eyes.

"Have one," Shanks urged.

Dulcedo held up an arthritic hand. "All that is behind me
now."

"Why?"

"Doctor's orders."

"Surely longevity can't be a goal at your age."

"I don't want to commit suicide, either."

"What is the latest word on the golf course murder?"

Others of the group began to arrive, jollying Debbie as they
came in, lowering themselves slowly and sometimes painfully
into their chairs, barking for a waitress so they could order
drinks. When this had been done, the question about the murder on the golf course was raised anew. Bruno, of course, had
news.

He insisted on their undivided attention. He licked his lips and rolled his agate eyes. And began. The police had, in the interest of thoroughness and because they had few leads to go on, checked out the golf bags of Sadler's three roommates.

Bruno's tablemates waited impatiently, but his eye was on the waitress approaching with his beer.

"So what did they find?"

Bruno drank deep and wiped his mouth with the back of his hand.

"Golf clubs," Shanks said disgustedly.

Bruno smiled as one in possession of as yet undivulged information will smile. It was a mark of the Old Bastards' table that each of its occupants sought to bring some scoop to the meal and dole out what he knew as slowly as possible. Bruno was merely following the conventions of the group.

"They found bottles of water."

Shanks sputtered into his manhattan. "Find me a golf bag without a plastic bottle of water in it and I will exercise daily for a week."

"Contaminated water?" Bruno asked.

"Contaminated!"

"Poisoned. And with the same poison that did in their roommate."

This was news indeed. Bruno sat back and allowed his fellows to worry the bone he had thrown them. The obvious thought was that someone had intended to wipe out all four of the old friends.

"But who?"

"That woman."

But Bruno did not intend to lose his role as master of the revels.

"Only one of the other bottles had the poison."

"Whose?"

Bruno pretended to search his memory. The waiter returned and the others began to place their orders, ignoring Bruno. He cried out, "Toolin."

"Who?"

"Christopher Toolin."

The others, having already accorded Bruno the reaction he deserved for bringing them this item of news, now acted as if the name of Toolin added nothing to the story. Bruno began to babble desperately, but he had lost his audience. In any case, his information was limited, passed on to him by Dennis Grantley as they walked toward the club from the 11:30 Mass at Sacred Heart. Bruno was a daily communicant. He visited the Grotto once a day. He wandered among the tombs in Cedar Grove, pausing at the markers of fallen colleagues. He longed for the untroubled faith of his youth but all he knew was dryness. He picked up his glass of beer and brought it to his full chapped lips, his pouched eyes sad. The Old Bastards had equivalently killed the messenger.

PART TWO

TOOLIN WAS INFORMED BY JIMMY Stewart of the results of the test performed on the water bottle taken from his bag. He stared at the detective in disbelief.

"In *my* bag?"

"Any idea who might have done that?"

"But I don't carry water in my bag. I bought a Coke." While they had waited in vain for Sadler to arrive, Toolin had bought a Coke and that was what he drank throughout his round.

"The others had water bottles in their bags."

"They bought those in the clubhouse."

"No doubt that was why theirs were not poisoned."

"My bag hasn't been out of my sight since I checked it at the airport."

"Where do you usually keep it?"

"At the Minikahda Club. In Minneapolis. Someone must have put it in my bag there."

"Who?"

"I have no idea."

He could not imagine anyone wanting him dead. That was more incredible than the poisoning of Mort. Again he thought of the last time he had been with Mort, the argument that

Crown had overheard. An awful thought crossed his mind. Mort had decided to kill himself and to take his old roommate with him, using the same means.

"It was the same poison?" he asked Stewart.

"That's right. Any ideas?"

He could not bring himself to voice the thought he had had. But even as he kept silent, he could imagine Crown or Barley remembering old animosities dating from student days. He and Mort had been forever quarreling about one thing or another. Mort had been a fussy person who objected to Toolin's habit of leaving clothes strewn around the room. Mort had slept in the loft they constructed in the room and a day usually began with him surveying the messiness below him and bellowing in anger at Toolin. It was an awful way to begin the day: that badgering, righteous voice, the one Mort managed to get into print when he wrote those silly articles for *The Observer*. Toolin's only defense had been to cover his ears with his pillow. From time to time there had been a scuffle. Once Mort even threatened to move out and leave the other three to the squalor caused by Toolin. They had begged him to stay, Toolin most of all, promising to be neat as a pin in the future, and for a week he had been reasonably conscientious about hanging up his things.

How childish those memories seemed, yet called up in the present context they seemed so much more. And Crown would certainly tell the police of the quarrel he had overheard when he came back to Mort's suite for a nightcap.

"I can't believe it," he said to Stewart.

"You seem to have a common enemy."

"We used to tell Mort he was his own worst enemy." That was as far as he was willing to go.

"In what sense?"

"Who knows? We just said it. That was long ago."

"I'm counting on you to give me some help."

"I wish I could."

"He may strike again."

" 'He'?"

"Do you think it's a woman?"

"No!"

"I've heard a lot about the war between Sadler and Maureen O'Kelly when they were students."

"Sure. When they were students."

"They seemed to renew it, didn't they? The golf bet?"

"That was stupid. She is twice the golfer he is." He paused. "Was."

"He even had a fight with her husband."

"Who told you that?"

"His nephew, Paul."

"Sam's son?"

Stewart hesitated. Perhaps he thought it was a biblical reference.

"Dr. O'Kelly took a swing at Sadler because he said something uncomplimentary about his wife."

"That was in Minneapolis."

"Were you there?"

"It happened in the locker room of the club we all belong to. The Minikahda."

"So you do know Dr. O'Kelly?"

Stewart stood, looking satisfied, as if he had made a point. Toolin sat back and looked across the lobby of the Morris Inn. In a corner there were bookshelves filled with old textbooks and volumes of *Reader's Digest* Condensed Books. A National Catholic Research University, indeed. Ben Barley came down the stairs to the left of the books and Toolin waved him over.

"Have you heard?"

"Nobody could ever kill you with water," Barley said.

18 ⟶ PHIL KNIGHT DROVE OVER TO
Holy Cross House to report to Father
Carmody. The discovery of the bottle of poisoned water in
Christopher Toolin's golf bag had complicated matters. Jimmy
Stewart felt under no obligation to pass on what had been
found to the press but some chatterbox downtown had decided
that the public had a right to know. It would be all over the
local paper in the morning and Father Carmody had to be
forewarned. When Phil left the Morris Inn, a van from a local
television station was pulling in. The fat was in the fire. He
thought of Roger and considered phoning him and telling him
of this development, but there was no rush. Phil had a prior
obligation to Father Carmody.

There are rest homes and there are rest homes, and on any
scale Holy Cross House would rank high, but that only made
it the lesser of evils. Or the least of evils. Like most men in the
full vigor of health, Phil felt ambiguous whenever he entered
the place. Old priests drooped in wheelchairs. In the television room, a therapist was leading a half dozen of them
through a series of exercises. Raise your right hand, raise your
left hand, put your arms straight out before you. One or two
simply ignored these commands, perhaps unable to comply.

Others obeyed and seemed to take a pathetic pride in their ability to do so. Would the day come when he considered lifting his arms an Olympic event? He hurried past the nurses' station and down the corridor where Carmody had his room.

The door of the room was open and Father Carmody was snoozing in his chair. For a moment he looked as old as anyone else in the house, but his eyes snapped open when Phil knocked on the doorjamb.

"I was just thinking of you," the priest roared, stirring in his chair. He got up and looked as if he might touch his toes and do a few push-ups. "Come in, come in."

The room was redolent of tobacco smoke, a sweet and pleasant smell. Father Carmody still smoked a pipe, but only in his room, largely because the practice was frowned on by the nurses and he needed to distinguish himself from residents who were ill and cowed into doing what they were told.

"They are wonderful women," he had explained to Phil. "Kind, considerate, all that, but bossy."

"It's a smoke-free campus," Phil reminded him.

"Bah!"

Phil told him of the poisoned water that had been found in Christopher Toolin's golf bag.

"The plot thickens. How do you explain it?"

"Jimmy Stewart is working on it."

"You must stick close to him, Phil. You know my concern."

"I'm afraid the media have already got hold of this."

Carmody said something Phil did not understand. Roger had explained that the priest always swore in Latin lest he give scandal.

96

"I want to talk with young Toolin."

"Young Toolin?"

"Chris. Everyone seems young to me. I had a little chat with him at the golf course yesterday morning, but that was just trivia. What has his reaction been?"

"Well, he canceled an appointment that would have taken him back to Chicago."

"Of course. Has it been decided where Sadler will be buried? From Sacred Heart, I suppose. Chris will have to stay for that."

"But Sadler lived in Minneapolis."

"Oh, they can bury him anywhere. But we must give him a Notre Dame send-off."

Just when Phil thought he was getting used to Catholics, a remark like that would remind him what an outsider he was. Roger's conversion to Catholicism had seemed at first only one more eccentricity, but Phil had come to see how profound the change in his brother had been. In some ways it was a barrier between them, but coming to Notre Dame had in large part removed it, because of the constant availability of sports. Phil supposed that he had come to think of Catholicism as athletic prowess. And then would come a remark such as Father Carmody's about giving Mortimer Sadler a five-star funeral from the campus church.

"Of course, they may want him buried here. I hope not. There are still plots in Cedar Grove but there is no way we can bury all our alumni on the grounds."

Phil mumbled something. He might have been speaking Latin.

"Well, that's up to the family. You say Mrs. Sadler is on her way?"

"That's what I'm told. The daughters will drive."

"Good. Good."

"I don't suppose we could have kept the threat to Toolin quiet for long."

Father Carmody made a dismissing gesture. He was less interested in what might have been than in what must be done. He picked up the phone and called the Morris Inn and asked for Chris Toolin. When he reached him he more or less ordered him to report to Holy Cross House.

"It's just across the lake. You can walk. It'll do you good after the scare you've had."

He listened for a moment, then hung up.

"No need for you to waste more time here, Phil."

Going out to his car, Phil felt that he had been dismissed.

19

FATHER CARMODY'S CALL CAME just after Maureen's to let Chris Toolin know that her daughter Francie had gone off for the evening.

"One of her professors invited her, isn't that nice?" There was a naughty lilt in her voice.

"Good for him."

"Well?"

"What would you like to do?"

"Do you have a car?"

"A rental."

"Good."

In the circumstances, it was hard to share her insouciance. When they had spoken of having time together if both came to Mortimer Sadler's rump reunion—her phrase—his conscience had easily been overcome, but now with Mort dead and the discovery of a bottle of poisoned water in his golf bag, Chris Toolin found it difficult to recapture the excitement he had felt when they had made their plans. But even with these unexpected events, he found the prospect of an evening with Maureen irresistible. For more than a month, ever since he had called her after Mort triumphantly gave him the news that Jack O'Kelly had moved out, they had been inching toward a renewal of a relationship that had marked their senior year. A platonic relationship, of course, although there had been walks around the lake and warm kisses in the twilight. He felt an almost boyish excitement now in remembering those long-ago trysts. How innocent they seemed. But innocence had not characterized their planning to meet at the reunion. Nor had the fact that Francie would come with her mother altered matters.

"She will be dying to get away from me, and I will make her feel guilty about it but let her go."

He asked if they should meet in the lobby in an hour.

"Better in the parking lot."

"Right." Discretion is the better part of hanky-pank. But he could not regard his renewed love for Maureen as something naughty. It was as if the promise of a quarter century ago was being fulfilled.

But then had come Father Carmody's call. With great reluctance he rang Maureen's room and told her he had to go over to Holy Cross House.

"Now?"

"Come with me. I'll drive and we can just go on from there."

"What on earth does he want?"

"He has heard of the discovery of the water bottle in my bag."

"Oh for heaven's sake." She had dismissed the news when he told her of it earlier.

"You'll enjoy it, Maureen. Father Carmody is a great old character."

"Isn't Holy Cross House the retirement home?"

"Yes, but he's not ill."

Her reluctance was evident, but she agreed. An advantage of the visit was that there was no need to avoid meeting in the lobby. Should anyone ask, their destination could only seem appropriate.

"I'll need fifteen minutes, Chris."

"That's all right. He thinks I'm walking over."

Twenty minutes later she came down the stairs into the lobby, a vision of impossible beauty. He went to meet her and whispered, "I've waited a quarter century for this."

"To visit Father Carmody?" But she squeezed his hand when she said it.

He drove south to the new campus entrance and there had to persuade the guard to let them through. Father Carmody's name was the open sesame. As they circled the area where the new dorms stood, among them the Sadler Residence, neither spoke. It was as if they were waiting for the familiar campus to reveal itself. And so it did when they passed the Rockne Memorial and then continued along the lake road. The Grotto was ablaze with votive lights, and Chris found himself wanting to ignore its reminder that the two of them were up to no good. He turned left, passed Dujarie House and then went on until they were able to get onto Douglas Road and reach the entrance to Holy Cross House.

"Chris, I'll wait in the car." She looked at him with a pained expression. "I just can't stand the sight of a houseful of old men."

He nodded. "I'll be as quick as I can."

"Oh, it's peaceful here. I don't mind waiting."

He leaned toward her and she gave him a cheek to kiss. He hopped out and went to the house and entered through the sliding doors. At the nurses' station, he was given directions to Father Carmody's room.

"You made good time," the old priest said, shaking Chris's hand and peering in his face. "Who wants to kill you?"

"Good Lord, I don't know."

"Sit down, sit down. Can I get you anything?"

"Father, before you called I made a dinner engagement . . ."

"Of course, of course. Anyone I know?"

"An old classmate."

The priest nodded approvingly. "That's the thing. Don't let this get you down."

Chris had been shaken by the news of the bottle found in his golf bag, but even so he was not prepared for Father Carmody's assumption that his life was in danger.

"Think of it, man. Sadler is found poisoned and the same kind of poison is found in your water bottle."

"But it wasn't my bottle."

Father Carmody ignored this. "Your other roommates were not targeted. Of course that raises an interesting question. Do you by any chance remember Dennis Grantley?"

"The golf coach?"

"Exactly. Now, he said something to me when we were talking of what happened to Sadler. His candidate was Ben Barley."

"Barley!"

"Why do you suppose he would think a thing like that?"

"Didn't you ask him?"

"At the time, I was trying to get rid of him. Now with this new development, and given the fact that Barley seems immune to threat, the remark returned. What do you think?"

"I think Grantley must be nuts."

Father Carmody chuckled. "You could make a case for that. Frankly I was surprised that he even remembered Barley."

Chris was very conscious of Maureen waiting in the car. Had he been dragged over here only to hear the speculations of an aged golf coach?

"Father, it's a preposterous idea. Of the three of us I would say that Barley was the closest to Mort Sadler. The two of them got together regularly. I know of absolutely no basis for the suggestion that Ben would harm Mort."

"Or you?"

"Father, I see Ben maybe once a year. We're old friends . . ."

He tried to imagine Ben Barley poisoning Mort and trying to poison him. It would have been far less preposterous if it had been Crown. He had been creeping around last night, eavesdropping on the exchange between Chris and Mort. He immediately rejected the thought. He shook his head, violently.

"None of us would dream of harming the other."

Father Carmody beamed. "Of course not. So it had to be someone else."

"That's right."

"Who?"

"I haven't the faintest idea."

"Very well. But I want you to give the matter some thought. The sooner this is cleared up, the better for Notre Dame."

He felt that he was escaping when he left the old priest's room and when he got into the car, Maureen noticed he was upset.

"That bad?"

On the way to Niles, he told her about the conversation and she listened in silence.

"Do you know what I think?"

"What?"

She hesitated. "I think it was Mortimer Sadler."

That made more sense than thinking it was Ben Barley.

20

WHEN PATRICIA SADLER GOT OFF the plane from Minneapolis with her daughter Vivian, Paul was there to meet them. Patricia took her nephew in her arms.

"I can't believe this has happened."

Paul patted her back, then held her close, saying nothing. Vivian looked on, silent and solemn. While they waited for the baggage to appear, they stood side by side, aunt and nephew.

"Your father will come tomorrow, Paul."

"Good."

It was as if they were both acknowledging that Samuel Sadler was not only the oldest son but now the undisputed head of the family, a role he had hitherto relinquished to his brother. Mort was the practical one; he had taken over the family insurance agency and brought it to new heights of prosperity; he was the director of the Sadler Foundation and had proposed the gift to Notre Dame that resulted in a residence hall that bore the equivocal name The Mortimer Sadler Residence, named ostensibly after their father.

"Why not just Sadler Residence Hall?" Paul had asked his father.

"Your grandfather's name was Mortimer."

"But that's my uncle's name as well."

"There has always been a Mortimer in the family."

Aunt Patricia now said, "The other girls are going to drive down in the van. Of course they had to arrange for babysitters."

Three of Paul's older cousins were married and had children. Vivian was the youngest and, being his age, the one he knew best. His aunt told him that the husbands would, of course, come for the funeral.

"It doesn't have to be here."

"Paul, it's what he would have wanted."

A light began to flash and then the carousel started to move. When his aunt pointed out their bags, Paul retrieved them, and then they were on the way to his car. When they were under way, his aunt beside him, the still-silent Vivian in the back, she said in a controlled voice, "Now tell me all about it."

As he talked, Paul managed to adopt his aunt's attitude toward her husband. This was a trick he had learned whenever her father came up when he and Vivian talked. Mortimer Sadler immediate family clearly had no idea what a shit he was, but then it was his treatment of his brother Sam that enraged Paul, and it was received opinion in the family that good old Sam enjoyed playing second fiddle to his younger brother. The sad thing was that this was true. By all rights, it should have been his father who annoyed Paul, not his Uncle Mort.

"When I got the call I had the distinct feeling that they thought Mort had killed himself."

"That's no longer the theory." And he told her of the bottle of poisoned water that had been found in Chris Toolin's golf bag.

"Oh, thank God he didn't drink from it."

At the Morris Inn, she and Vivian registered and his aunt thanked Paul for meeting her plane. He turned and Vivian came into his arms.

"Francie's here."

"I know."

"That will make it easier."

"Yes. Mom and I will have things to do now, you know," she said in a low voice.

"If I can be of any help . . ."

"Paul, you've been wonderful." And his Aunt Patricia once more took him in her arms and began to cry. She was still crying when the elevator doors closed on her and Vivian.

Outside, Paul stood under the canopy and looked beyond the university club to the ugly silhouette of DeBartolo, a classroom building. He lit a cigarette and strolled to one of the benches across from the entrance to the Morris Inn, where he sat and tried to feel the peacefulness of the campus. There was a lull between sports camps now, and it was a relief not to have to face a hall full of squealing kids. He had taken the summer job at Notre Dame in order to be away from Minneapolis, but the arrival of his uncle had reminded him of all his grievances against him. He had skipped the last meeting of the family foundation, e-mailing his judgment of the applications, giving a thumbs-down to those he thought his uncle might favor. Sitting there on the bench outside the Morris Inn, finishing his cigarette, he wished he hadn't said to Francie

107

what he had about his uncle. She had enough family troubles of her own.

His memories of his mother were achingly tender, and he loved his father for settling into the life of a widower. Francie's parents sounded like a couple of kids, always squabbling. Maureen O'Kelly was just too attractive for her own good, and she couldn't resist coming on to men. Some feminist. Did she lead men on in order to act indignant when they responded? Paul had felt her power himself the day she showed him around her flower garden. She seemed to want to be her daughter's rival. Now she was separated from Francie's father and despite Francie's confidence that the breach would be healed, Paul sensed her dread that her mother was going to try to be a girl again. Not that Dr. O'Kelly was much better. It was Maureen's suspicion about him and Laura Kennedy that had precipitated the breakup. Good God, the man must be sixty years old.

"Laura is the same age, Paul," Francie had said.

Old people talked about the foolishness of the young but what of their own acting up? Paul, of course, thought the force that through the green fuse drives the flower must abate with age, to be followed by serenity and rectitude. He had begun to wonder if perhaps temptation continued to the grave.

21 ---------→ DENNIS GRANTLEY'S ROOM ON the second floor of the firehouse was as austere as a Carthusian's cell. Over the years, he had progressively discarded his possessions until now a few hangers in the closet were sufficient for his clothes, a single bookshelf held a small selection of golf instructional manuals and as-told-to lives of a dozen professional golfers. His television had gone on the blink, and he got rid of it and did not replace it. The pharmacopeia that had been his father's was the one reminder of his parents, a kind of family bible. His radio was tuned to WSND, the local FM channel that featured classical music and, on weekends, Brother Pedro playing golden oldies and commenting on them in his cracked confiding voice. An easy chair, collapsed and comfortable under a lamp, and a single bed over which hung a color photo of the Golden Dome, a dresser for shirts and shorts and socks. He looked around his room with a judicious eye. Could he pare his life even closer to the bone?

No miser ever derived more pleasure from the acquisitive impulse than Grantley did from liberating himself from the tyranny of possessions. His golf cart belonged to the university; his car was twenty-five years old. Members of the Congregation of Holy Cross took the vow of poverty, but Grantley warmed himself with the thought that he was poorer than any of them. The one thing he had not acquired was poverty of spirit. He was proud of the bareness of his room. Even as he drank Father Carmody's Irish whiskey he silently condemned the priest for having it.

His room was, he realized, the counterpart of his life, of his soul. In the Gospel story, when the devil was driven out and the heart swept clean of his presence, a new danger loomed. The expelled devil returned with others worse than himself. Now, whenever he said the Lord's Prayer, Grantley felt under judgment.

He attended daily Mass, he said his rosary at the Grotto, he wandered from campus eatery to campus eatery, living well within his monthly social security check. He had never touched his retirement fund, his intention being to bequeath it to the university. It was his dream to endow a chair and live on as the donor of the Dennis Grantley professorship—in what? That was his problem. Maybe, as Father Carmody had suggested, he would consult Roger Knight. His choice must be carefully made because his generosity was motivated by spite: He would leave a significant sum of money to Notre Dame as a rebuke for the treatment he had received. Was he any better than Mortimer Sadler?

When he had told Bruno of the discovery of the water bottle in Chris Toolin's golf bag, he had been confident that Bruno would spread it far and wide.

"Come have lunch at the club, Grantley," Bruno had said as they walked across the campus.

"I'm not a member."

"Why not?"

"I can't afford it."

Bruno had fallen silent and when they parted, Grantley had watched Bruno shuffle off to the entrance of the club, preening himself on the thought that he was not like the rest of men. He was content to taken his meals in the LaFortune Student Center, in one of the dining halls, or in one of the many eateries now scattered across the campus. His one indulgence was drink and he preferred the bar in the Morris Inn. Of late it had given him a vantage point on the investigation into the death of Mortimer Sadler.

Sadler had been a lousy golfer, whereas Toolin could have been good if he had put his mind to it. At Warren yesterday, Toolin had glanced at Grantley sipping his coffee but had not recognized him. Ben Barley had looked over twice and then come to his table.

"Weren't you a coach?"

Grantley nodded. He had given Barley instructions in golf years and years ago.

"Simpson?" Barley asked, then rejected the guess. "Moran!"

Grantley had merely smiled.

"I never forget a name," Barley said.

Grantley watched him with a malevolent eye as the man rejoined the others. Barley did not call their attention to the man he had misidentified as Moran and Grantley took mordant pleasure in being ignored.

The three men were standing impatiently on the first tee

when Grantley came out, their bags all in a row. They would be waiting for Sadler. So word had not reached them that they must play as a threesome in the tournament. Eventually, Grantley got behind the wheel of his golf cart and drove silently away toward Douglas Road.

That was yesterday. Now, as darkness gathered in his scarcely furnished room, he did not turn on the lamp beside his chair. From the radio came Bach's "Air for the G String." He had his small revenge on Barley when he told Father Carmody that of the old roommates it was Barley who was most likely to have done Mortimer Sadler harm.

22 FRANCIE MET VIVIAN IN THE Lobby, taking her hands in hers and silently conveying what she could not find words to say.

"Let's go for a walk."

They headed for the Main Building, the Golden Dome already lighted and shining in the gloaming, down to the Grotto, where Vivian knelt. She is praying for her father, Francie thought. Her father is dead and she is praying for the repose of his soul. Suddenly, the horror of what had happened came home to her. She knelt beside Vivian and for the first time prayed for Mortimer Sadler.

Afterward, they walked along the lake path and Francie told Vivian what she had been doing.

"Roger Knight is here and he has been so good. We must go see him." Francie felt magnanimous in suggesting this. Sometimes she thought that she and Vivian were rivals for the role of Roger Knight's pet.

Vivian nodded. "I'd like that." She turned to Francie. "I can't believe that someone killed my father."

"The police will find who did it."

"But what difference will that make?"

Francie was uneasy with the thought that the police seemed

to think her mother could have had something to do with Mortimer Sadler's death. That was ridiculous. She would have preferred to think that Vivian's father had committed suicide, if the thought weren't so awful.

"Now I wish we had called Roger Knight."

"I have my cell phone."

"Should we call him? His brother is taking part in the investigation."

"Oh, I don't want to talk about that. I've been trying not to think about it. Isn't that terrible?"

"Give me your phone."

"I hope the battery isn't dead."

The phone rang and rang, and Francie was about to give up when Roger answered.

"Knights."

"This is Francie! Vivian has arrived. We're walking around the lake and suddenly had the idea to call you."

"A splendid idea. Let me talk to her."

"We were hoping to come over there."

"Even better."

And so they reversed direction and headed for graduate student housing, where the Knight brothers had their apartment. Roger stood in the front door as if he had been waiting for them. He reached out for Vivian's hand and soon she was enveloped in his arms, sobbing her heart out. Francie looked on, feeling almost jealous. Roger had never hugged her.

Once they were inside, Vivian brightened as Roger steered the conversation away from her father, instinctively knowing that was the thing to do.

"Has either of you read Trollope?"

Vivian immediately perked up. "The Palliser novels."

"Of course, of course. They are wonderful, although of the series I prefer the Barsetshire novels. But it is the so-called minor ones that have a special delight. I have been reading *Kept in the Dark*. Not for the first time, but I can't remember enjoying it so much before."

He went on and on and it was wonderful. He made popcorn and insisted that Vivian have a beer, so Francie took one, too, and they settled down for more discussion of Trollope. They had been there an hour and a half before Roger turned to what had happened to Mortimer Sadler.

"Who might have done such a thing, Vivian?"

"My mother's first thought was my uncle Sam, but that is silly. He's in Minneapolis."

"Paul's father?" Francie asked.

"He is the elder brother, but he never acted like it. Now he will have to."

"Why would your mother have had such a thought?"

"It's a long story."

Roger settled back. "Well?"

And so Vivian told them about the Sadler family. Her grandfather had established an enormously successful insurance agency as well as the Sadler Foundation, and it was her father, Mortimer, who had been his successor, despite being the younger son.

"My uncle taught philosophy."

"I look forward to meeting him."

"He should be in tomorrow."

"Your mother must have imagined he resented playing second fiddle to your father."

"Oh, but he didn't. It is Paul who resents it. And I understand. I would feel the same way if I were him. But my uncle is one of the most contented men I know. He took early retirement and, being widowed, lives like a recluse on Lake Minnetonka. I think he reads as much as you do."

"A philosopher," Roger said wonderingly. "I have always envied philosophers."

"Isn't your degree in philosophy?" Francie asked.

"That does not make one a philosopher."

"My uncle is a Thomist," Vivian said.

"Oh, I really do want to make his acquaintance."

"Now he may have to take a more active role, at least in the foundation. At least until Paul graduates. Paul is everything his father isn't."

Roger insisted on taking them back to the Morris Inn in his golf cart. Francie let Vivian sit beside him and took the seat behind that faced backward. She listened to Roger talk and watched the campus slip away behind them, the little puddles of light under the lamps succeeding one another at intervals. Thank God they had called Roger Knight. Vivian was almost her own self again.

23

WHEN JIMMY STEWART HEARD that the widow of Mortimer Sadler had checked into the Morris Inn, he and Phil came to talk to her. Vivian joined her mother and Roger and Francie took chairs in the lobby. Two glasses of wine had made Francie voluble and she spoke to Roger about Paul Sadler.

"Why is he on campus?"

"He's working here this summer, in the sports camps. And taking a course in botany."

"Is that his major?"

"No. He just likes it. I tried to interest him in your course last spring, but he was afraid."

"Afraid?"

"I shouldn't have told him so much about you."

"That would frighten anyone."

Because she could tell Roger Knight anything, Francie told him the sad story of her parents' separation.

"So there is a real Laura?"

"Laura Kennedy."

"Your father's undergraduate sonnets were dedicated to Laura. I had thought he was taking over Petrarch's beloved as well as his sonnet form."

She said, "Greg Whelan found them for me in the archives."

"So you've read them."

"I can't. I began but I couldn't go on."

"I understand."

And Francie was sure he did, although she was not so sure she herself did. The poems had been written before her parents had even met, but it was impossible for her not to read them in the light of later events.

"Sleep tight," he said when he rose to go.

She wanted to lean toward him and kiss him on the cheek, but she didn't. Such displays of affection had become so commonplace as to be meaningless. That was why she kept Paul at arm's length. She dreaded to enter into a more decisive phase with him. The two of them seemed carriers of all the troubles of their respective families, as if they bore some virus that would affect them with the folly of their parents.

Francie was still awake when her mother came in, but she feigned sleep, reluctant to enter into a midnight conversation. The sound of her mother's humming as she moved around their darkened room, the only illumination coming from the windows, was not cheering. She found herself praying that the death of Mortimer Sadler would not further fragment both her family and Paul's. The story of her father striking Mortimer Sadler had at the beginning the note of gallantry, but it had proved to be the catalyst for the separation of her parents. Francie drifted into sleep, her lips moving in prayer for herself, her parents, for Paul, and for poor Mortimer Sadler, dead on the golf course of the university he had so crazily loved.

24

GHOSTLY LIGHT PLAYED UPON the ceiling of Chris Toolin's room, where he lay on the bed, his hands behind his head, reviewing the evening like a lovesick boy. Maureen had been charming, affectionate, confiding, if sometimes disturbing.

"Thank God they found that water in your bag, Chris."

"Oh, I wouldn't have drunk it. I hate bottled water."

"So you told me. But it takes me off the hook."

"How so?"

"Of course, the police thought I was responsible for Mort's death. Cherchez la feminist. I never made a secret of what I thought of him."

"They could never seriously think you would so such a thing."

"No? Why wouldn't I?"

"Oh, come on."

"Of course they will learn, if they haven't already, that I am a gardener. I have some deadly nightshade in my garden."

"Is it uncommon?"

"Well, you have to grow it on purpose. And be very careful kids don't get near it."

"Is it beautiful?"

"Not really."

"Unlike the gardener?"

She put her hand on his and he felt enveloped in her smile. Her gesture changed the course of the evening. They had dined well at the Carriage House and were aglow with wine when they left. When they entered the elevator at the Morris Inn, it was understood that she was coming to his room. He felt a sudden panic at this fulfilment of his wildest hopes. But instead, their time in his room had been a continuation of their conversation at the restaurant.

"What was it that Mort said to your husband?"

"He suggested that I was running around. Jack's reaction was prompted more by his own guilt than anything else. He took a swing at Mort in the locker room of the club and caught him on the side of the head. It knocked him to the floor. I could have cheered when I heard about it." She paused. "Not from Jack."

"What do you mean, guilt?"

"Jack has renewed an old liaison with Laura Kennedy. She was at St. Mary's when he was here. They would have married if Jack and I hadn't met. Sometimes I think he felt unfaithful to Laura all along."

Chris didn't know what to say so he said nothing. He took her in his arms when she said she must go and their kiss was passionate. But she stepped away.

"I want to be in the room when Francie returns."

"Of course."

"She may be already there. I told you she was going to spend the evening with one of her professors."

"Ah."

"Better that than Mort's nephew."

"I don't understand."

"Paul Sadler. The son of Mort's brother, Samuel. She thinks I don't know and I think if I don't make a thing of it she'll get over it."

"Boys don't get over things so easily." He held her hand. "Nor do men."

Her meeting Jack O'Kelly had spelled the end of their undergraduate romance as well. It was an odd thought that he owed the renewal of their relationship to Mort. From Mort he had learned of Maureen's separation from her husband and the reunion had provided an opportunity for this evening.

"When will I see you again?" he asked before opening the door.

"Whenever you want."

She gave him a hurried kiss on the cheek and was gone, and now he lay on his bed, reliving the evening, a wistful smile on his face.

But it was impossible not to see what they were doing in the light of his reaction to her accusation against her husband and Laura Kennedy. Nor could he avoid the aching sense of guilt he felt when he thought of his own long-suffering invalid wife. At least in the case of the O'Kellys, each retained the possibility of a life without the other, but his wife, Ruth, was wholly dependent on him physically and emotionally. His only justification for what he was doing was that it was merely a fling, nothing that threatened any permanence. Did he even in his heart of hearts imagine that Maureen saw him as her future?

25 ROGER'S INTENTION TO SLIP UN-
obtrusively into the Galvin Life Sci-
ences Center the following day to talk with Professor Jacob
Climacus was thwarted when his entry into the building
brought everyone in sight to a standstill. They stared at the
enormous visitor, who blinked back at them, smiling cherubically. It was like pausing a movie on the DVD player while
one went to the kitchen. When Roger moved toward the
reception desk, the others resumed their comings and goings
but a half dozen followed in his wake, curious.

"I've come to see Professor Climacus."

The woman looked up at him with rounded eyes as if the
better to take in his bulk. She put her hand on a phone.
"Whom should I say is calling?"

"Roger Knight. He is expecting me."

"Ah."

An undergraduate was recruited to lead Roger off to the
hothouse where the professor of plant biology spent his days.

Roger was not surprised to find Paul Sadler there. He lifted
a hand in greeting and was led to a little man seated on a stool
who looked up at Roger over his glasses.

"Good day," Roger said.

"Good Knight?" A wry smile seemed to form beneath the grizzled beard.

"I have come to pick your brain."

"That is more than I got to do. I accepted the one that was issued to me."

" 'Issued from the hand of God the simple brain'?"

Discolored teeth appeared among the foliage of the beard. "Milton?"

"Wordsworth. Is there another stool?" Roger looked up and down the rows of plants that flourished fiercely in the heat of the glassed-in addition to Galvin. Climacus wore sandals, suntans, and a T-shirt damp with perspiration. He rose.

"Let's go into my office. If you're not used to this place you're likely to melt."

"Could you show me around first?"

Paul Sadler seemed to have disappeared. Climacus led Roger up and down the narrow aisles of his domain, now touching a leaf, now admiring a bloom, several times leaning forward to whisper to one of the plants. He turned to Roger.

"Talking to them does help, you know."

"Do they ever answer?"

Climacus made a sweeping gesture. "This is their answer—just being the best they can be."

Stories about Climacus had come to Roger over recent years and it had always been one of his hopes to meet the professor of plant biology. Now, with the death of Mortimer Sadler, he had reasons other than collegial curiosity to look him up.

Climacus's office was just off the hothouse and its contrasting chill elicted a sneeze from the professor. Climacus removed some pots from a bench and pulled it toward his desk.

"This should accommodate you." Climacus went around the desk and sank sighing into a chair, then took a package of cigarettes from a desk drawer. He offered one to Roger, who refused. Climacus lit up, inhaling with obvious delight.

"You realize that I am conducting an experiment on the tobacco plant. This is a smoke-free campus." The beard adjusted to his smile.

"Of course. Tell me about poisonous plants."

"Almost all plants are poisonous to some species of animal."

"And humans?"

"We are rational animals."

"More an ideal than a description, I'm afraid. Have you heard of the death on the golf course?"

"Only what you told me on the phone."

"The man was poisoned. With deadly nightshade."

Climacus looked pained. "A much-maligned plant. Like hemlock. Poisonous plants often have great medicinal benefits. But that is as incidental to them as their harmful effects. Of course, we ingest vegetation and other animals but that is our doing, not theirs. The harmful ones have been known from time immemorial, discovered by hit or miss. Nowadays, we classify and rename them, but by and large we are codifying the folklore of centuries."

"But surely not all are equally harmful."

"When I go into a house I always notice the plants, of

124

course. A good portion of them are lethal. Poisonous effects are a plant's way of protecting itself."

"Teleologically?"

"Of course. Don't believe all the nonsense you hear about science. A purely mechanical explanation of a plant suggests that its mature state is a happy accident, happily repeated. Nonsense. The plant is present in the seed because the seed has come from another plant. The point and purpose of seeds is to perpetuate a species. If that is teleology, let my enemies make the most of it."

Roger laughed. "Surely you have no enemies."

"Other than poisonous plants? No. But talk to me about Milton."

Thus it was that Roger, having been assured that the species of plants provided a veritable cornucopia of poisons to one who knew their properties, found himself discussing Milton with Climacus, who proved to be remarkably knowledgeable.

"My interest was inspired by the line in *Lycidas*: 'To sport with Amaryllis in the shade.' "

"A lovely line."

"The amaryllis is a lovely plant."

"I think the poet meant a girl."

When Roger eventually rose to go, he had made another friend. He and Climacus had agreed that the professor of plant biology must come to the Knight apartment for dinner at his earliest convenience.

"I should tell you that I am not a vegetarian," Climacus said.

"I should hope not."

26

LATER THAT DAY, PHIL TOLD Roger of Jimmy Stewart's reaction to learning that Maureen O'Kelly was a renowned gardener. A phone call to Minneapolis, requesting discreet inquiries, had turned up the fact that Maureen had several deadly nightshade plants in a special fenced garden in her yard devoted to herbs. Motive and means being established, the question became one of opportunity. How could Maureen, or anyone else, for that matter, have put the bottle of poisoned water in Mort Sadler's golf bag?

"The answer is, easily. He had dropped off his bag at the first hole of Burke the night before his fatally interrupted practice round."

"But how would she have known?"

Phil shrugged. "That is the question."

Roger could not help but think how this affected Francie. "It all sounds pretty speculative, Phil."

"Oh, Jimmy isn't likely to make any accusations on what he has now. Of course, he will be pursuing it."

"Will you go with him?"

"Yes."

"Keep me posted, won't you?"

"You don't seem to like the possibility."

"All your theories are based on the assumption that the water bottles were put into the bags here."

Phil just stared at Roger, who went on. "They brought their golf bags here, didn't they?"

"What are you suggesting?"

"Only what I'm saying."

"Bah."

After Phil went off to meet Jimmy Stewart, Roger did the dishes and tried not to think of what his brother had told him. The only way to counter Maureen as a possible suspect was to produce an alternative. The suggestion that the victims had brought the poisoned water with them to Notre Dame was a logical possibility. But so many things are. And then, after he had turned on the dishwasher and shuffled off to his computer, he remembered Paul Sadler's interest in botany. The boy had been in the hothouse, confirming that interest. This suggested a possibility hardly more welcome than Maureen O'Kelly. To wonder about Paul was also to affect Francie, who obviously liked the lad. But an additional factor was Francie's account of Paul's dislike of his uncle Mort as they sat in the lobby of the inn.

"Why?"

"Oh, it's a family thing. And he blames Mort for the trouble my parents are having."

Then she had told him of the episode when Jack O'Kelly had angrily struck Mort to the ground for some insinuation about his wife.

The married state was a mystery to Roger and never more

so than when there was a falling out of spouses. His memories of his own parents were doubtless affected by his sense of melancholy loss, but in his recollection they had been entirely devoted to one another. He could sympathize entirely with Francie's sense of desolation when she spoke of her parents' separation.

"I said a rosary at the Grotto, praying that everything will be all right again between them."

And now Jimmy Stewart was actively pursuing the possibility that Francie's mother was responsible for the death of Mortimer Sadler.

Five minutes later, Roger called Francie at the Morris Inn.

"Thank you for a lovely evening," she said.

"I enjoyed our conversation." But even as he said it, it seemed to Roger that, apart from her confiding about Paul, he had done most of the talking. When he mentioned d'Aurevilley's novel *Le prêtre marié*, she had wanted to hear all about it and he had obliged.

"I can't wait to take that course."

"I can't wait to give it."

Roger had already checked the summer course schedule, remembering that Francie had said Paul Sadler was enrolled in a course in botany. There was only one, and it ran for most of the morning, doubtless involving a lab.

"Are you free now?"

"What's the plan?" she asked with a lilt in her voice.

"I thought I would come by for you in my golf cart and we could just roll around campus and talk."

"Wonderful."

"In half an hour?"

"Perfect!"

It was a glorious day, with the late morning sun filtering through the trees and squirrels scampering about. In the Lobund Laboratory generations of germ-free mice had been raised for experimental purposes, while on campus, unmonitored and uncontrolled, squirrels had over the generations become fearless of humans and were always on the qui vive for offerings of food. Roger detoured by the Grotto and smiled at the visitors who were feeding ducks near the lake. These ducks, too, were almost domesticated, their food supply in large part coming from people who brought sacks of bread which they scattered among the feathered beasts. The Canada geese, nobody's favorites, did not receive the benefits of this preferential option but eventually they would enter with awkward strutting into the ceremony and chase the ducks away.

On the road, Roger followed the great circular road up and past the Rockne Memorial and maintenance shed and then turned off toward the Morris Inn, driving past the row of new residences, one of which was Sadler Hall. The building had indeed become a memorial now, sooner than its donor must have expected.

Francie was waiting under the canopy at the entrance of the Morris Inn and hopped in when Roger pulled up in his golf cart.

"Where are we going?"

"The campus is at its most beautiful. It's a shame so few students get to see it as its best."

He crossed the road, got onto the sidewalk, and they went

past the law school into the main mall. As he drove, Francie went on about what he had said of the campus in summer.

"It was one of my motives for coming with my mother."

Her mention of Maureen O'Kelly strengthened Roger in his resolve. "Your friend Paul is one of the lucky ones."

She laughed. "You remembered his name."

"Perhaps because of his family name. How is he taking his uncle's death?"

"I think I told you that he was not a great fan of Mortimer Sadler."

"You did."

"Families are complicated things."

"He lives in Morrissey, doesn't he?"

"I didn't tell you that."

"I looked it up."

"You did!"

"Francie, I want you to humor me. I want to take a look at his room."

"Whatever for?"

"I asked you to humor me."

"All right." But her expression was a puzzled one.

At the hall, they went inside, and Roger drew her attention to the portrait of Joseph Evans, the first director of the Maritain Center. He tapped on the rector's door. A rumpled, barefoot young man in a sweatshirt and suntans answered.

"Hello, Father."

The priest stepped back. "You're Professor Knight."

"And you are Father Green."

"No, he's away. I'm sitting in for him this week. No heavy duty with nothing going on."

"This residence isn't used for summer programs?"

"Not this week, thank God."

"What is your name, Father?"

"Casperson."

"C.S.C.?"

"Yes."

"This is Francie O'Kelly. We have an unusual request. Paul Sadler is living here, right?"

"He is."

"We have been deputized to get something from his room and neglected to ask him for the key. Could you let us in? It would only take a minute."

"Of course."

"How did you know who I am?"

"You're a legend."

"Am I? I had no idea."

"I'm stationed in Portland and stories about you reach us even there."

"Well, well."

Father Casperson took some keys with him, led them to the elevator, and punched the button. Soon they were rising to the third floor. The priest stepped out and they followed him down the hall, where he unlocked a door, opened it, and looked in. When he stepped aside, Roger remained in the open door and looked around. What he had guessed was a window box on an earlier reconnoiter past the residence proved to be just that.

"Father, could you see if there is a copy of Plato's *Republic* on the desk?"

The priest entered the room and searched for a minute, then turned with disappointment. He shook his head. "I'll check the shelves."

"No, that won't be necessary. I can't thank you enough."

So down they went again, Roger satisfied with the expedition, his two companions clearly mystified. Having thanked the temporary rector, Roger and Francie returned to the golf cart.

"What was that all about?"

"You will probably think that I lied to Father Casperson."

"Did Paul send you for a book?"

"If you think of it, you'll see I never quite said that."

"Just implied it?"

"A venial sin at most."

"What was the point of that?"

"I wanted to see what a typical student's room looked like."

"Are you lying again?"

"Not at all."

"But there's something you're not telling me."

"That's right. Let's continue our tour."

A glance had sufficed to verify the suspicion that had brought Roger to Morrissey. The window box had contained two types of plant, each easily identifiable. One was marijuana. The other was deadly nightshade.

27

ROGER WAS IN AN AGONY OF
doubt. When his hunch about Paul
Sadler had proved right—seeing the window box in the third-floor window of Morrissey had led to his visiting the residence
with Francie—he found himself reluctant to act on the discovery. The kind of investigation in which he engaged with Phil
was easier when the problem was abstract, almost algebraic,
with the actors like variables in geometry, A and B and C. But
the death of Mortimer Sadler had taken place on this campus
he had come to love, and it involved persons who were more
or less known to him, some well known, like Francie O'Kelly.

It had been the desire to divert suspicion from her mother
Maureen that had set Roger's mind on a search for an alternative. Francie's mention of the hatred Paul felt for his uncle
had been put forward as just a family thing, but that did not
prevent Roger from wondering if the nephew had been the
cause of his uncle's death. His intention, the first time he
drove his golf cart past Morrissey, had been to visit Paul, but
the glimpse of the window box had kept him moving along the
walk toward Lyons Hall. The later visit, exploiting Father
Casperson and confusing Francie, had confirmed his worse
fears. But what must he do now?

The obvious answer was to give the information to Phil and let the chips fall where they may. But before he did that, he confided what he had found to Greg Whelan.

"Marijuana?"

"It is the deadly nightshade that is relevant."

"Perhaps."

"You think it just a coincidence?" There was a little leap of hope in Roger's ample breast.

"If it is and the marijuana is found, he is in big trouble."

"There is only a plant or two. Luxuriant plants."

"One would be enough to cause him trouble."

"Then you don't think I should tell Phil?"

"I wouldn't say that. At least that doesn't bring the police into it right away."

"I'm afraid you don't understand the obligations of a private investigator."

"But you're a private investigator."

That, of course, was the rub. In one sense, he had no choice as to what he should do. What he had discovered in Paul's room could scarcely be considered irrelevant to the investigation into Mortimer Sadler's death. Roger was trying to take refuge in a technicality: It was Phil who had been engaged by the university, not he. But that wouldn't wash. However informal his cooperation in the case might seem, Roger was his brother's partner, privy to what had already been found. There was no need to imagine Phil's indignation if he sought to conceal what he found in Paul Sadler's room. Indignation would not adequately express what Jimmy Stewart would feel.

"I guess I am just putting off the evil day."

"Why don't you talk to the boy?"

Of course. Roger beamed. How right he had been to come to Greg. If there was a connection between Paul Sadler's window box and his uncle's death, let the boy come forward on his own. Prompted, of course, by the realization that the nature of his gardening was known.

"Good man!"

Going down in the library elevator, which he shared with a library minion and a cart of books to be reshelved, Roger found himself checking the titles on the cart. The employee had on a headset and was listening to who knew what on the CD player hooked to her jeans. How could one do such a job without wanting to look into each book before returning it to the shelf? The girl smiled vaguely, whether at Roger or at what she was listening to was difficult to say. The door opened and Roger indicated that she should go first. She shook her head.

"Oh, I'm going up."

"You didn't want to go down?"

"It doesn't matter." Again the vague smile.

The doors closed and Roger stood watching the indicator above the door as the car rose to the thirteenth floor. Did she ride up and down out of boredom, to put off her task? It seemed a symbol of his own vacillation. He hurried away. He did not want to be there when the car returned and learn whether the girl and her cart were still on it.

———

He had parked his golf cart on the west side of the library and when he went out to it, Paul Sadler was seated behind the wheel.

"Paul!" He had been introduced to the boy by Francie and, given the burden of his thoughts, recognized him immediately. "Just the man I want to see."

"So Father Casperson told me. I was sure this was your cart."

His plan had been to enlist Francie and arrange a meeting with Paul, but he was glad now that he did not have to involve her. Roger, with an assist from Paul, got into the passenger side of the cart and handed Paul the key.

"Where to?"

"Anywhere. We can talk as we ride."

Paul put the cart in reverse and backed away, then shifted and they were off. The walks were filled with teenaged girls and their mothers, on campus for a flag-twirling convention, so Paul took the road that led past the Center for Social Concerns toward the firehouse. Roger was considering how to begin when Paul spoke.

"You visited my room."

"Yes."

"You should have called first."

"I did. I wanted to make sure you weren't in."

Under the bill of his baseball cap, Paul frowned straight ahead. Roger went on: "I had noticed your window box from below and wanted to get a look at it."

Paul paused at a stop sign and then continued north. When they came to a barrier, the arm lifted and Paul drove on.

"Have you told anyone?"

"What would I tell them?"

"What you discovered."

"It is the significance of what I discovered that matters."

"You think I killed my uncle."

"Did you?"

"No." But he had hesitated before he said it.

Was this the sort of toying with the truth he himself had been guilty of with Father Casperson and Francie? "I didn't kill him, the water did"? As Lord Jim might have explained his desertion of the *Patna* by saying that he hadn't jumped, his feet had.

"If that is true, there's an end to it."

"You don't believe me."

Paul was hunched over the wheel as if their speed was considerably more than ten or fifteen miles an hour.

At Douglas Road they were held up by traffic, but then they crossed and continued along the road past the Credit Union.

"Where are we going, Paul?"

"You said just drive."

It occurred to Roger that if Paul were lying—and that seemed almost certain—he was in a possible predicament, riding away from the main campus in this way. Ahead were the great fields used for parking on football days, now uneven expanses of grass. Paul bumped across them and came to a stop under the shade of a tree. They were in the middle of a vast field, visible enough if anyone were about but far from any actual witnesses. Above them, a plane descended slowly toward the airport, its wheels lowered. Paul turned to Roger and pushed back the bill of his cap.

"You could get me into a lot of trouble if you tell anyone what you found."

"Deadly nightshade."

Paul seemed surprised. "I mean the marijuana."

"You could get rid of that."

"I got rid of the entire window box. There's nothing to be found anymore."

"I see."

"But you could still say what you saw."

"For many reasons, I would rather not."

"But you will."

"Tell me about your uncle."

"I didn't like him, if that's what you mean."

"Why?"

Paul lifted his hands from the steering wheel as if he were about to pray, then dropped them. "I wouldn't know where to begin. It has to do with my father."

"Tell me."

As Paul spoke, Roger felt his difficulty increase. It was impossible not to sympathize with a son who thought his father ill treated by his uncle.

"Not that he ever complains about it. He couldn't have been so marginalized if he hadn't allowed it."

"And now he is the head of the family whether he likes it or not."

"He will probably want me to take Uncle Mort's place."

"Ah."

"You'd have to know my father to understand."

"Is he coming down?"

"That might have been his plane landing just now."

Roger's apprehension at being with the one he thought might have killed Mortimer Sadler had dissipated. Was to know all to forgive all, after all? But how could he overlook what he suspected Paul of having done? What if neither Father Casperson nor Francie had noticed the window box? He had not drawn attention to it, but rather asked the priest to look for a copy of *The Republic* on Paul's desk, choosing a title he was certain would not be there.

"So what do you want me to do, Paul?"

"Nothing."

"That is asking a lot. I am a private investigator, you know."

"Who hired you?"

"The university asked my brother to monitor the investigation for them. And we are partners."

"Would you mention the marijuana?"

"No."

Paul looked relieved. "Then there's nothing to tell. Do you know who gave me the deadly nightshade seeds?"

"Who?"

"Mrs. O'Kelly. Francie's mother."

"She did!"

"Yes."

"Why?"

"Oh, she just talked about what an interesting plant it is. And it is. But you can see why I don't want it mentioned."

"Tell me." But Roger felt a renewal of dread.

"I took her to my room to show her the plant."

A simple sentence but fraught with implications. Paul did

not have to spell out what his own fears and suspicions were. But he did.

"She took some of the berries and a leaf or two."

"Maybe we should head back."

"Are you going to tell all this?"

"I wouldn't know what to say."

And that, he considered, as they went back across the bumpy field toward campus, was the truth. Maybe not the whole truth, but the truth.

28

HER MOTHER WAS SPENDING THE afternoon with a woman she described as a townie, a classmate who had settled in South Bend with her family and who had come to pick up Maureen, certain she could not follow the directions to her house. Alone, Francie had tried not to imagine what the point of Roger Knight's mysterious visit to Paul's room had been. But she couldn't avoid the thought that it had something to do with the death of Mortimer Sadler.

Vivian was busy with her mother, which was just as well. Francie felt a need to be by herself, but she had no inclination to sit alone in a room in the Morris Inn, brooding. The keys to the rental car were on the dresser and Francie thought of their golf clubs, hers and her mother's, in the trunk of the car. This suggested a way to while away the time.

She went downstairs and out to the car, drove to the campus entrance, and talked her way past the gate guard.

"I'm going to golf," she told him.

"If you want Warren, it's over on Douglas Road."

"No, I want the old course."

He waved her through, and she drove to Rockne and found a parking place beyond the building housing campus security.

She popped open the trunk and hesitated. Her mother's clubs were on wheels. Francie's plan was to go out to what had once been the sixteenth fairway and hit a few balls. She got her mother's clubs from the trunk and soon was heading out the ninth fairway, keeping to the edge because there were golfers approaching the tee. Five minutes later she had reached the truncated sixteenth, now a practice hole.

It was when she unzipped a pocket to get out some balls that she found the plastic bag. Curious, she took it out and held it to the light. The berries were bright and the leaves still fresh looking. An awful thought occurred to her when she realized where she had seen such leaves before: in her mother's herb garden at home. Deadly nightshade.

More thoughts roared through her mind like the cars of a train. She actually looked around, boxing the compass, fearful that she was being observed. She was about to stuff the plastic bag back where she had found it when it struck her that it would be the equivalent of pointing a finger at her mother. In a moment she made up her mind.

She took a sand wedge from the bag and hurried to the fence that separated the fairway from the extension of Cedar Grove Cemetery. She chopped at the turf, pulling away the grass and making a hole. Then she dropped the plastic bag into it, covered it over, and stamped the spot with her shoe. It was like repairing a divot. When she hurried back to her mother's golf bag she felt that now the two of them shared a terrible secret. She dropped a ball, improved the lie with the sand wedge whose face was caked with dirt, then swung deliberately, striking the ball. It rose, describing a perfect arc and then fell. Short of the green.

"Where have you been?"

"I went out to hit a few balls."

"Alone?"

"Yes."

"Hasn't Vivian called?"

"I'll call her."

"Not right away. Francie?"

She turned to her mother, but avoided meeting her eyes.

"I love your father, Francie. The separation wasn't my idea."

"Was it his?"

"He thinks he is in love with Laura Kennedy."

"Did he really knock Mortimer Sadler down?"

"Yes!" There was the thrill of pleasure in her mother's voice. But she added, in a somber voice, "Little did I realize that that was the beginning of the end."

"Because of Mortimer Sadler?"

"I suppose you could say that."

"Would you?"

"It's as good as an explanation as any."

"And reason enough to kill him?"

"Francie! Your father would never harm a single soul."

"I don't think he would."

"How I wish your father were here now."

"Why don't you ask him to come?"

"Would you?"

The prospect of her parents' reunion was a powerful incentive. She telephoned her father in Minneapolis.

"Come to South Bend!" he cried. "What for?"

"Mother is in trouble, Dad. Serious trouble."

"What kind of trouble?"

Francie turned away from her mother as she told him. Mortimer Sadler's death. Police questioning. "They're harassing Mom." It seemed a pardonable exaggeration. She wanted her mother to seem in need of her father's support. He did not interrupt. Afterward, he was silent. Then, "I'll be down as soon as I can."

Her radiant smile when she turned to her mother answered the question in Maureen's eyes.

It was a moment when she might have accused her mother, told her what she had discovered, told her what she had done with the plastic bag filled with parts of the poisonous flower. But by burying it, she had already entered into a pact of silence. Whatever her mother had done, Francie knew she would never be the one to accuse her.

"Now I am going to call Vivian. We may go do something."

"Oh, good."

29

DENNIS GRANTLEY SAT AT A COR-
ner table in the bar of the Morris Inn,
Agnes Walston across from him, gazing soulfully into his eyes.
In street clothes, Agnes had shed her persona as long-time
waitress at the Sorin Restaurant in the Inn, and on this, her day
off, was (as she put it) all gussied up and dying to see the town.
The prospect of an unsettling evening did not appeal to Grantley. He had accepted Agnes's flirtation for years and managed
to keep the woman under control. Agnes had metamorphosed
from divorcée into widow, thus removing the convenient
impediment of a husband. Of course, Agnes had not been dis-
suaded in her ardor by Grantley's exaggerated account of the
retirement package a grateful university had conferred upon
him. She thought he was kidding when he said he had a room
in the firehouse.

"There are great new steakhouses out on Grape Road and
Main Street."

"The mall? I can't drive a golf cart out there."

Agnes giggled. Whenever Grantley spoke the truth she
thought he was kidding even as she accepted his prevarica-
tions as gospel truth.

"We can take my car."

"I'm not a gigolo."

"What's that?"

"What I'm not."

She let it go. One of her assumptions was that Grantley's long stay at Notre Dame made him an intellectual and that meant he could say unintelligible things from time to time. She sat back and arranged her décolletage, not an exercise in modesty. She wore a black suit and the jacket was not unlike the effect of Grantley wearing a suit coat without a shirt. A lot of Agnes was on display, and Grantley felt half-remembered stirrings of concupiscence. But if she was an occasion of sin, it was a remote one. Grantley's few excursions into the mysteries of the flesh had taken place years ago and all he remembered was the shame afterward, increased by the need to confess his transgressions, receive absolution, and be restored to the ranks of those who had a fighting chance of getting into heaven.

"Are you Catholic, Agnes?"

"Only on Sundays. Most Sundays," she added.

"What kind of name is Walston?"

"It was my husband's name."

"What was your maiden name?"

"Chorzempa."

"What kind of name is that?"

"Polish."

She had been raised on the west side of South Bend, once an ethnic stronghold with Poles and Hungarians in large supply, their rival churches standing shoulder to shoulder.

"You still live on the west side?"

"Nobody lives on the west side anymore."

Agnes had a condo in a development so close to the Toll Road that she was serenaded to sleep by the constant roar of semis not a hundred yards from her pillow. This was Grantley's reconstruction of her complaint.

"You should move."

"Into the firehouse?"

"Ho ho."

In an effort to divert her mating instinct, he brought up the recent campus murder. Agnes had the anonymity of a waitress in Sorin's and picked up all kinds of gossip; diners assumed she was part of the decor as she came and went in her uniform, always with an ear open. Maureen O'Kelly usually took a table in Agnes's section and Agnes had become fascinated with the blond bombshell, as she called her.

"She's been a busy bee since checking in."

"How so?"

Agnes leaned forward, about to talk, then sat back. "I'll tell you at Houlihan's."

"Where's that?"

"Out on Main."

Grantley hesitated. If he let Agnes take him off in her car, he would be at her mercy, and there was a new determination in her attitude as if she meant for him to fish or cut bait. She wasn't getting any younger. Well, who was?

"You're faking."

"Maybe." But she smiled enigmatically and Grantley was hooked.

"Where's your car?"

"In the lot."

"Let's have another drink first." His voice even sounded coy.

"We can have a drink at Houlihan's."

As he followed her through the lobby, Grantley felt oddly like a trophy. At the front doors, she waited for him to be gallant and he obliged her, pushing through first and holding the door. Outside, she led him to the parking lot and a Corvette.

"What's this?"

"Do you like it?"

"I've never ridden in one."

"It's snug. You'll like it."

Going out Notre Dame Avenue, Grantley felt a sense of adventure. He seldom left the campus and, as he had said, he had never been in a car like this. He felt like Robin to her Batman.

If Father Carmody could see him now!

The noise level in the bar at Houlihan's did not provide a promising setting for any confidences Agnes might have. The dining area was better and he suggested that.

"There'd be a wait. I thought you'd want to watch a game."

A dozen television sets brought in half a dozen different athletic contests, the lower part of the screen conveying in text the inane remarks of the commentators. Agnes wanted to sit at the bar, but Grantley headed for a booth, tripping on the step that led to its raised level. He managed to right himself and Agnes slid in beside him. He felt trapped.

A waitress came and Agnes ordered a beer of enormous proportions. Grantley asked for scotch and water, and the waitress was off.

"Isn't this wonderful?" She put her arm through his and leaned against him.

"Tell me about Maureen O'Kelly."

Agnes wrinkled her made-up nose. "Later. You won't hear a word I say in here."

"So why did we come here?"

"Silly." Her arm squeezed his.

For two and a half hours they drank and had enormous hamburgers served with enough potato chips to satisfy the most voracious appetite. All Agnes's appetites were on display. As she ate, she licked her lips and gave him her soulful look. She was like the squire in *Tom Jones* as she laid into her food. She gnawed suggestively on a spear of pickle. On his third scotch and water, Grantley felt his defenses weaken. Agnes looked better all the time. He didn't even resist when she suggested that they adjourn to her condo where the hum of the semis was less distracting than the dozen television sets in Houlihan's.

Agnes's condo was a pleasant surprise and Grantley was struck by the contrast with his room on the second floor of the firehouse. He could live like this if he wanted, but that would entail leaving the campus and he doubted he could bring himself to do that. There was a deck, on the opposite side to the Toll Road, and they sat there, having yet more to drink. The immediate future seemed vague and oddly welcome. *Que sera sera.*

"So, what about Maureen O'Kelly?"

"Who cares?"

"I do."

"Why?"

"I should have known you had nothing to tell."

"Oh, but I do."

"Oh, sure."

Agnes pulled her aluminum chair closer to his and they sat knee to knee. "She's got something going with the one named Toolin."

"How do you know?"

"Wilfrid, the night clerk. They came in late the other night and went up in the elevator, close as can be. Wilfrid went up the stairs and saw them come out of the elevator and go to his room."

"Big deal."

"For a couple hours he kept ringing her room and didn't get an answer."

"It probably doesn't mean a thing."

"Listen, a woman knows."

"Is Wilfrid a woman?"

"They had breakfast together the next morning. I could tell."

"Ah."

"Well, you wanted to know."

She put a hand on his knee and he put his hand on hers. "Agnes," he began. She turned her hand over, gripped his, and pulled him to his feet. A minute later they were in her bedroom. Who knows what might have happened if there hadn't been a picture of the Sacred Heart on the wall? Grantley freed his hand.

"I've got to get home."

"You expect me to drive you back now?"

So they had an argument. He ended by sleeping on the couch in the living room, Agnes having closed the bedroom door with an angry bang. On the Toll Road the semis thundered all night like voices of conscience. Grantley tried to pray, glad he had not sinned, but he couldn't stop thinking of what Agnes had said about Maureen O'Kelly and Christopher Toolin.

30

ABSTRACTLY CONSIDERED, THERE
was no question in Roger's mind what
he should do, but what he had learned was far from abstract.
There was, of course, the possibility that Paul was lying about
Maureen O'Kelly taking leaves and berries from the plant he
had grown in his window box. But that did not present an
attractive alternative. His dilemma was that he had information that he should not keep to himself, but if he told Phil he
would in effect be accusing either Paul or Maureen O'Kelly.
Roger was in a state of uncharacteristic confusion when he
went out to his golf cart and drove to Holy Cross House to talk
with Father Carmody.

He found the old priest in a lawn chair that faced the lake,
dozing in the sun. Across the lake, through the trees, was the
silhouette of the old campus, the Golden Dome, the spire of
Sacred Heart Basilica rising to the blue June sky. Roger
pulled another chair next to the old priest's and sat. A rheumy
eye opened and regarded him.

"Roger."

"Father. You know Aquinas well, don't you?"

"Tolerably."

"I have been thinking of the text in which he writes of the

family of a man condemned to death. Am I right in remembering that he held that their blood relationship takes precedence over their duty to justice?"

"Ah, an interesting conundrum."

"I have been wondering what other considerations might trump the demands of justice."

Father Carmody looked out toward the lake and sat straighter in his chair. He might have been putting on a stole.

"What is it?"

So Roger told him, as he would have told a confessor, what he had discovered in Paul Sadler's room and what Paul had told him of Maureen O'Kelly.

"And what will you do, Roger?"

"What would you advise?"

"You are wondering if you must make this known. I mean to someone else."

"Yes."

Father Carmody ran his hands down his cheeks, turning his face into a tragic mask.

"And it was your previous impression that Mrs. O'Kelly did not know of Paul?"

"Her daughter had not revealed her feelings for Paul. But I suppose she must have known the name, and perhaps the person."

"Did the young man say why she had come to see him?"

"To see his window box."

"And how would she have known that?"

"It was she who got him interested in belladonna."

"How much of his story do you believe?"

"Ah, that is the question."

"Perhaps your doubt is justification enough for saying nothing. At least for now. Let me see what I can do."

"You mean you will tell Phil?"

Father Carmody smiled. "Not now, certainly. There is someone else I must talk to."

And so it was that Roger returned to campus, somewhat relieved. He stopped at the library and took the elevator to the sixth floor, where he found Greg Whelan at work in the archives.

"Roger, what a delightful surprise." Heads turned at the sound of Greg's uncharacteristically fluent voice. "There is something I want you to see."

Greg led Roger off to a study room, closed the door, and eased onto the table the archival box he had been supporting on his hip. He sat and pulled the box toward him, his expression that of a child opening a Christmas gift. His fingers flew over the tabs of the manila folders the box contained until he found the one he sought. He pulled it out, opened it, and slid a photocopy across the table to Roger.

It was an article from *The Observer* of a quarter century ago, recounting how Mortimer Sadler had been whisked away to the emergency room at St. Joseph's Hospital to have his stomach pumped.

"Poison?" Roger said.

"Not just any poison."

Mortimer Sadler had fallen ill from the ingestion of belladonna. His roommate, Christopher Toolin, had had the presence of mind to call an ambulance immediately when he found Sadler collapsed on the floor of their room in St. Edward's Hall.

"Well, well."

"Things happen once as farce and the second time as tragedy."

"Isn't it the other way around?"

"Not this time."

Greg slid another, later story across the table. This made it clear that Sadler had administered the poison to himself. Unwittingly, as he claimed. But there was an ambiguous quote from Toolin: "The poor devil missed a chemistry test."

Roger recalled an allusion to this from Jim Crown during his interview with Phil and Jimmy Stewart. He pushed his chair even farther from the table than his midsection required and smiled cherubically at Greg.

"I can't tell you how happy this makes me."

"Happy?"

"Well, not happy. But it comes as a tremendous relief."

And then he hunched forward and told Greg in a whisper what he had just been discussing with Father Carmody.

"Suicide is an awful possibility, but these stories suggest that Sadler had simply wanted to get out of his bet with Maureen O'Kelly. As he had before, he underestimated the danger of what he was doing."

"And that takes Mrs. O'Kelly off the hook."

"And Paul." Roger sighed. "And your humble servant, I might add." He rose in careful degrees to his feet. "Could you make me copies of these? I want Phil to see them."

"Of course."

It would have been an exaggeration to say that it was a lighter Roger Knight who descended in the library elevator some minutes later, save metaphorically. He was humming as he came out of the car on the first floor.

31

THE WOODEN BEADS OF HIS rosary slipped through Dennis Grantley's fingers as he sat on a bench at the Grotto, but if his words flew up, his thoughts remained below. He had just come from confession, but he did not feel the relief that absolution usually brought. He had agonized over whether he should confess his date with Agnes as carelessness about the occasion of sin, but any mention of it would have conferred on it more importance than it had. Nothing had happened. He could not even accuse himself of sins of thought. His main concern had been to escape Agnes's predatory advances and in this he had succeeded, to the point of her disappearing into her bedroom and slamming the door. This left him stranded far from campus, which was why he spent the night on her living room couch. But why, if he was sinless, did he feel such guilt? He worried that his confession had not been a worthy one since he had not mentioned Agnes.

He had awoken to the sound of the shower and her tuneless singing. When she emerged, she was wearing her waitress uniform. She seemed surprised to see Grantley in her living room.

"You stayed the night!"

"You will remember that we came here in your car."

"Oh, sweetie, I'm so sorry." A lascivious smile. "You might have knocked on the bedroom door."

He ignored this. She was aglow from her ablutions and a picture of propriety in her uniform, whereas he was a rumpled mess with a furry mouth and an uneasy conscience. While she made breakfast, he went to the bathroom and stared at his whiskered face in the mirror. What might have happened if he had knocked on the bedroom door? Out of danger, he could enjoy imagining the possible upshot. He gave himself a look. Shame on you. But he felt a bit like a roué when he went out to his bowl of cornflakes.

Agnes had dropped him off at the firehouse and he went up to his room, but all he could think of was that confessions were heard in the basilica prior to the 11:30 Mass. He had been the first in line, whispered the usual menu of his sins through the grill. Now, an hour later, he sat at the Grotto wondering if he had come clean to God and his minister.

Someone sat next to him on the bench. He turned to face Father Carmody.

"Finish your rosary," the priest said.

Fear and hope leapt together in Grantley's breast. He could confess to Father Carmody and undo the possible sacrilege of his earlier confession. But the difficulty recurred. What exactly could he accuse himself of? He pocketed his rosary and piously blessed himself.

"Now then," Father Carmody said. "You know everything that goes on around here."

"You flatter me."

"I accuse you. You are a magpie of gossip; news sticks to you as flies do to flypaper. What do you know of the doings of those members of the class of 1977 who are here for a reunion?"

Grantley thought about it. What surer route to a recovered sense of innocence than to accuse others?

"So you've heard about Maureen O'Kelly and Chris Toolin."

"If I had, I wouldn't be pumping you for information."

"It probably doesn't mean anything," Grantley said in a tone that implied the opposite.

Carmody glared at him. "Don't be oblique. What are you talking about?"

Grantley opted for directness and told him what Agnes had found out about Maureen's going to Toolin's room in the Morris Inn. "After midnight," he added.

"As you say, it probably means nothing."

Grantley stared at the votive lamps flickering in the cavern of the Grotto. Our Lady, the epitome of purity and innocence, gazed down on him. "Or they could be in it together."

" 'It'?"

"The poisoning of Mortimer Sadler."

"Why?"

"In her case, it's obvious. There was enmity between him and the woman."

"Don't abuse Scripture."

"And she was Eve to his Adam."

"You're not making sense."

But it was clear to Grantley that Father Carmody had taken

159

to heart his interpretation of the midnight tryst of Maureen O'Kelly and Christopher Toolin, co-conspirators up to no good in the night.

Father Carmody got to his feet. "You are a reservoir of iniquity."

"And obliquity?"

"That too." Father Carmody went up the steps to the parking lot and his car. Grantley took out his rosary again and began to pray it with attention and devotion. He might have been saying his penance.

32 - - - - - → WHEN THE CELL PHONE WENT off in his briefcase, Cal Swithins at first had no idea what was happening. He was in his car at the time, parked in a lot at police headquarters, making notes for a dispatch to the *Chicago Tribune,* eschewing the press room lest the odious Raskow should be reminded of his professional duties. By the time he figured out that it was the phone Maddie Yost had given him, the better to have him at her beck and call, it had stopped ringing. With some difficulty, he managed to pick out the number of *The Shopper.*

"I tried to reach you," Maddie said without preamble.

"How did you know it was me?"

"Caller ID. Look, I want you to go out to the mall and get an extension from Boswell for his ad. Where are you now?"

"At police headquarters."

"They'll never run an ad." A pause. "Is something wrong?"

"Not if I get some rest."

"Rest! Rest from what?"

Recent events had brought home to Swithins the demeaning trough into which his career had sunk. Imagine composing a column for a virtual illiterate like Maddie Yost. But even worse was the fact that she considered him a space salesman, not a writer. Dear God. Swithins's persistent investigation of the death of Mortimer Sadler now carried the promise of lifting him from the jaws of defeat and putting him on a more exalted path than he had ever trod before. The *Chicago Tribune* had expressed interest in receiving his accounts of the strange murder on the Notre Dame campus. Chicago was the home of vast numbers of Notre Dame alumni, and the city's population could be evenly divided into those who loved Notre Dame and those who hated her. Either way, interest in such a scandal would be intense.

Swithins would not have been human if he did not imagine the reaction of Lyman Mendax to the news that the reporter he had rejected had been good enough for Chicago. At one end of the spectrum of his hopes, Swithins imagined himself the regular Notre Dame correspondent of the Chicago paper, feeding it daily dispatches on campus events. Not sports, of course. Platoons of sports writers descended on South Bend on game days and covered each event like a blanket. Swithins frowned at the cliché. He must keep his style fresh and innovating, but accessible. At the other extreme of hope was a summons to Chicago, installation in an office with the title of feature writer. His eyes narrowed in pleasant thought.

He was shaken from his reverie by Maddie's nagging voice.

"Go see Boswell before you collapse." Her voice was heavy with disbelief.

"Your wish is my command."

"That wasn't a wish."

She hung up. Swithins searched for and found the appropriate buttons on the diabolical little device that seemed a leash Maddie Yost had him on. (Dangling prepositions were okay in the demotic style to be cultivated.) He stuffed it back in his briefcase with symbolic violence. Boswell indeed. Boswell was fighting a losing battle with the big chains, trying to run a bookstore on the old model. The truth was, Swithins liked the place. He and Boswell had spent many happy hours in the back room, sipping red wine and reviewing the disappointments of their lives.

"Of course I want to write," Boswell had confided, sniffing. His nervous sniffing was a constant of his conversation. "That is why I envy you."

Ah, if Boswell only knew how that confession made him plummet in Swithins' estimation. The reporter had sufficient self-knowledge to realize that anyone who envied him was on a very low rung of the ladder of life indeed. Boswell had rummaged in a drawer and come out with a legal pad whose top sheet was covered with a penciled scrawl. "Notes for my novel," he said sheepishly.

Boswell ran a modest space ad in *The Shopper* that featured quotations from his favorite authors: Edna Ferber, Sinclair Lewis, John Bannister Tabb—choices that betrayed his age and his hopeless lack of fit in the contemporary scene.

Swithins drove to the mall and was soon ensconced with Boswell in his back room. Mrs. Hitts, his clerk, a deaf old lady who worked for peanuts out of love for books, minded the store.

"Of course I'll renew the ad," Boswell said. He seemed in a manic phase. "John Bannister Tabb has worked his magic. I have had an extraordinary visitor."

"Who?"

"You may not know him. Professor Roger Knight."

"But I do know who he is."

"He spent an hour with me." Boswell rolled his eyes in ecstasy. "We talked of everything." He sat forward. "He and his brother are investigating the murder at Notre Dame."

Swithins's belief in Providence came roaring back. Maddie's importunate call suddenly seemed less an interruption of his Chicago dreams than an integral part of the scenario.

"And what did he say?"

"Oh, we talked of poisons. The man is a thesaurus of trivia. Of the best sort."

"Do they have a suspect?"

"An old girlfriend, apparently. A classmate of the deceased."

"Maureen O'Kelly?"

"That's the one. But mainly we talked of John Bannister Tabb. I didn't realize he was a priest."

"Knight?"

"Tabb."

While Boswell reminisced about Roger Knight's visit, Swithins resumed composing in his mind his dispatch to Chicago. OLD CLASSMATE TARGET OF MURDER INVESTIGATION AT NOTRE DAME.

"What's that sound?" Boswell asked.

Swithins snapped out of it and looked at his briefcase. "I've got to go." He rose.

"Is it an alarm clock?"

"More or less."

33 WHEN THE HISTORY OF NOTRE
Dame is written, the names of the occu-
pants of the Old Bastards table in the university club are
unlikely to figure in it. Their academic careers had been
undistinguished, they had left little mark on the place where
they had lived out their days, yet in their own minds they were
the epicenter of local events. At lunch the following day, the
topic was the funeral of Mortimer Sadler, which had taken
place that morning in the basilica of the Sacred Heart. Only
Bruno had attended, and the others listened patiently to his
unnecessarily lengthy description of the send-off that had
been given a son of Notre Dame who had met his end in so
equivocal a way.

"Who preached?"

"One of the vice presidents."

A groan. The multiplication of those bearing that title was a
frequent topic of complaint at the table. There were now vice
presidents, associate vice presidents, and assistant vice presidents in obscene number.

"We've become a Mexican army—all generals."

Bruno regained the floor and attempted to give a resume of
the homily but was hooted down. None of the Old Bastards

had held a classroom of students in thrall, but they were convinced to a man that they could have given a better sermon than the superfluous vice president.

"And I didn't even know the dead man," Armitage Shanks said.

"Neither did the preacher," Bruno said. "It was a terrible performance. He thought he was addressing the widow but he was looking in the wrong direction."

"How did she take it?"

"Like Niobe, all tears," said Bruno, surprising himself with the remembered phrase.

"Was he buried in Cedar Grove?"

"He will be buried in Minneapolis."

"At least he had his funeral here."

Silence fell as each considered that he, too, had such an appointment in Sacred Heart if not in Samarra, God only knew how soon. It is a peril of longevity that one outlives those who might have mourned him or at least shown up for the funeral. A month before, one of their number had succumbed and the members of the table had distributed themselves around in different pews in Sacred Heart, trying unsuccessfully to create the impression of a good turnout. The deceased represented one fewer attendant at their own final obsequies. The thought had brought on unsimulated sorrow. But for whom else do we weep at funerals if not ourselves?

Armitage Shanks called them to order by asking if the murderer of Mortimer Sadler had been found.

Bruno looked wise. "If only I was at liberty to say."

"You are. Say it."

"The university has put Philip Knight onto the case."

"Who is he?"

"You know who he is."

"Remind me."

"The brother of Roger Knight."

"*Obscurum per obscurius*," murmured Angoscia.

"The fat endowed professor."

"Endowed with fat?"

"He too is a private investigator."

"A professor!"

"Before he joined the faculty. The two brothers worked together."

"And they named him an endowed professor?"

"The Huneker Professor of Catholic Studies."

"And they will solve the case?"

"The brother will."

"The other brother."

Debbie came sailing across the dining room to the table and pulled out a chair and sat. Her arrival drove gloom from the assembly and they all turned dentured smiles on her. But her manner was solemn.

"Have you heard?" she asked.

"What?"

"One of the students was taken to the hospital to have his stomach pumped out. He had the same poison in him that killed the man on the golf course."

Appropriate murmurs and cries of surprise.

"What is his name?"

"Sadler."

"No, no. The student. Sadler is the man who was murdered on the golf course."

Debbie got huffy, as if her story was being questioned. "Well, that *is* the name I heard. Sadler."

"The student?"

"Yes. Paul Sadler."

PART THREE

34

PAUL SADLER HAD MADE IT TO the elevator and descended to the first floor, which is why Father Casperson, hearing a weak scratching sound on his door, looked out and found the young man lying on the floor outside his room. His first instinct was to give absolution, after which he dashed to the phone and called 911. Next he called campus security. By the time he returned to Paul, he was certain Paul was dead, and he knelt beside him to pray. He was still kneeling there when the campus police arrived. They were followed soon after by the ambulance, and Father Casperson gave way to the paramedics, who were unsure what the problem was.

"Is he dead?" the priest asked in a strained voice.

"Not yet, anyway."

"Can I come with you?"

"Sure."

On the ride to the hospital, the priest spoke compulsively, saying that he had imagined filling in for the rector of Morrissey would be a restful stress-free time. He had never faced an emergency like this. As he spoke, his eyes never left Paul and his expression told what he dreaded.

In the ER, the doctor on duty assumed it was a drug overdose and ordered the patient's stomach pumped. This misconception saved Paul's life. Within hours, the poison in his system was identified. The police were notified at once, and Jimmy Stewart came, with the persistent Cal Swithins hard upon his heels. Stewart barred the reporter from entering the room in the ER where Paul still lay, awaiting transfer to a room in Intensive Care.

"How's he doing?" Stewart asked the nurse.

"You'll have to talk to the doctor."

He showed her his identification.

"You'll still have to talk to the doctor."

"Where is he?"

In reply, she pressed a buzzer and then left on squeaky running shoes. Paul's eyelids fluttered and Stewart leaned over him.

"What happened?"

The eyes opened. "Where am I?"

Stewart told him, adding what had been already done. "Tell me what you remember."

The story was hardly audible and less than coherent, interspersed with groans as Paul felt the effect of the stomach pumping. A doctor came in in the midst of this, and ignored what was being said. His name tag read ARINZI.

"Deadly nightshade?" Stewart asked him.

Arinzi nodded. "That makes two, doesn't it?"

"Three." Stewart got out his phone and punched a number. "Phil? Look, will you go over to the Morris Inn and have a talk with Maureen O'Kelly." He added a cryptic account of what had happened. "I'll meet you there."

174

As he was heading for the outside door, Swithins fell into step beside him.

"What's his name?"

"Ask the doctor."

"I'm coming with you."

"You're not under arrest."

"Ho ho. I know he was brought here from Notre Dame."

"I hope you can account for your whereabouts."

He slid into his car, and Swithins grabbed the top of the door and held it.

"You can't ignore the press."

"I wouldn't dream of it. Are you thinking of becoming a reporter?"

"I'm with the *Chicago Tribune*."

"I never read it."

Stewart pulled the door shut and Swithins let go before his fingers were crushed. He drove away as Swithins ran to his car. When he reached the first intersection, Stewart could see in his rearview mirror that the reporter was following him. He really didn't give a damn. It was ridiculous to think a thing like this could be kept a secret.

The boy was the nephew of Mortimer Sadler, who had died of poisoning four days ago, but what that meant Stewart could not guess. If they could discover why Mortimer Sadler had been poisoned, some explanation might be found. The best theory they had now was that an undergraduate grudge lay behind the death of Mortimer Sadler. That pointed to Maureen O'Kelly. But what reason could she have for poisoning the nephew as well as the uncle? If she had poisoned either. But at the moment, it was the only lead he had. He hoped Phil Knight had found Mrs. O'Kelly in the Morris Inn.

Dr. O'Kelly had come from Minneapolis but had registered in a separate room from his wife. Samuel Sadler was also in the Morris Inn, as were the daughters of Mortimer; Vivian stayed with the mother, the other girls in another room. Anger rose in Jimmy Stewart as he reviewed the events of the past days. But if he was angry to have poisonings going on in his jurisdiction, the most recent one seeming an almost personal affront, he could imagine what Phil Knight must be thinking. After all, his task was to protect the reputation of the university. Well, there was no way Notre Dame could avoid bad publicity now.

When he pulled into the parking lot of the Morris Inn, Swithins was riding his bumper.

35

THE NORMALLY SEDATE AIR OF the Morris Inn was again disturbed as Jimmy Stewart, with Phil Knight beside him, began once more to question those of the class of 1977 who had taken part in the reunion organized by Mortimer Sadler. They were joined now by family members who had come for the obsequies of the fallen alumnus. As news spread of the near-death experience of Mortimer's nephew, Paul, disquiet pervaded the lobby.

Roger Knight had decided to come to the inn after Phil received the call from Jimmy Stewart and dashed off. His thoughts were of Francie and Vivian as he directed his golf cart across the campus. The two girls had returned to what would normally have been the idyllic peace of summer only to be swept up in events that affected them poignantly. Vivian had lost her father, and Francie's mother was now the principal interest of the investigation.

When Roger waddled into the lobby, he created the usual stir with his massive presence. Mrs. Sadler with her older daughters occupied the couch and chair before the fireplace, but it was the man in the corner, frowning over a book, that drew Roger. Samuel was a spare man with a goatee and wispy mustache, his eyes blinking behind thick glasses.

"I am Roger Knight," he said, coming to a puffing halt before the seated man.

"Ah." The man rose and put out his hand. "Samuel Sadler. My niece has told me of you."

"Such sad events," Roger said, easing himself carefully into an inadequate chair.

"I am about to leave for the hospital to see my son." He lifted the book he held. "I found this on that shelf."

The book was an outdated textbook in electrical engineering.

"Why on earth is this on display?" Samuel said.

"How will you get to the hospital?"

"I suppose I will call a cab."

"In South Bend? Nonsense."

In a far corner, Jimmy Stewart and Phil were talking to a composed Mrs. O'Kelly. Roger told Samuel Sadler to wait and lumbered over to his brother.

"Phil, I must use the car."

Mrs. O'Kelly gave him a radiant smile. "You're Professor Knight."

Roger took her hand and she rose as if he had tugged at it. "Francie goes on and on about you," she said.

"She is a wonderful young lady."

"Thank you."

"Is your husband here?"

"He just checked in. He's in his room." Mrs. O'Kelly nodded her head at Jimmy and Phil. "I am being grilled by these two."

"Do you intend to drive?" Phil asked, with something like terror in his tone.

"Perhaps Samuel Sadler will take the wheel. We are going to the hospital to see his son."

Samuel joined them. Roger was surprised that he and Mrs. O'Kelly did not know one another. He bowed in a courtly manner to Mrs. O'Kelly when she identified herself.

"How dreadful about Paul," she said, touching his arm.

"More dreadful about Mortimer."

"Yes."

"It was an impressive service. There must have been a dozen priests in the sanctuary."

"A Notre Dame farewell," Roger said.

"What was that they sang at the end?"

"The 'Salve Regina'?"

"No, the English hymn."

"Ah. 'Notre Dame Our Mother.' "

"Beautiful."

"It brought tears to my eyes," Maureen O'Kelly said. "I don't know when I last heard it."

Phil said, "It is sung after every basketball game."

"Really?"

Phil asked Samuel if he would do the driving, and Samuel suggested that then there was no need for Roger to come to the hospital.

"But I want to talk with you."

Phil gave the keys to Samuel. "Be sure you drive."

"How will I know the car?"

"Roger can identify it." Phil told Roger where he had parked.

The hospital was ten minutes away, and Roger and Samuel exchanged small talk on the way. For the first time, Roger realized how tense Samuel was. Of course. He was going to visit his son in Intensive Care. But it was Mortimer he mentioned.

"It was the kind of funeral he would have wanted."

"Perhaps not so soon."

"Was Mrs. O'Kelly serious when she said she was being grilled?"

"Let's see Paul first."

The patient lay on his back, awake, staring at the ceiling. His face lit up at the sight of his father.

"Dad!"

"I thought you were boycotting your uncle's funeral." He leaned over the bed and kissed his son. "And to think it was this."

"I'm all right. So they tell me."

"You must come back to Minneapolis with me."

"Dad, I'm working here."

"They can release you. You must take it easy for the rest of the summer."

Roger Knight came forward, and Samuel explained his presence. "The police are talking with Mrs. O'Kelly."

Paul glanced at Roger. "I'm sure it's just routine."

"It is a strange feeling to outlive one's younger brother," Samuel Sadler said an hour later.

Roger had directed him to the apartment just east of campus when they left the hospital, suggesting that the Morris Inn would continue to be disrupted by the investigation into the poisonings, stirred to new heights by what had happened to Paul.

When Roger showed him his workroom, his guest moved reverently along the shelves. He looked at Roger. "No old textbooks here."

"There you're wrong. I still have the books that introduced me to the classics."

"Latin and Greek?"

"Latin and Greek."

"That's different. You have quite a collection of philosophy, too."

"My degree was in philosophy."

"So was mine."

"I've heard a bit about you, of course. I'm sorry we meet in such tragic circumstances, but I could not forego the chance to talk with you. Could I get you something to drink?"

"What are you having?"

"Don't be guided by me. I am a teetotaler."

"A matter of principle?"

"No, of conclusion. Alcohol doesn't agree with me."

"I have a long and deep understanding with it."

Roger poured his guest a generous measure of single malt scotch, opened a root beer for himself, and they settled down to talk. As will happen when kindred spirits meet for the first time, theirs was a wide-ranging and excited exchange during which they found they had many interests in common. But then came a lull and, inevitably, the death of Samuel's brother came up again.

"Roger, I can tell you now I was almost relieved that Paul, too, had become a target. I scarcely dared think this while he was in danger, but now I feel free to say it."

"It does look as if one and the same person is responsible for what has been happening."

"You don't sound completely convinced of that."

"I have learned to withhold judgment as long as possible in such matters."

Samuel sipped his scotch. "Maureen O'Kelly?"

"Does that seem possible to you?"

"Mortimer had a genius for both lasting friendships and lasting enmities. He certainly gave her reason enough to resent him. On the flight down, he went on and on about the speech she gave when they graduated."

"The flight down?"

"I flew down with Mortimer in his private plane the other day."

"You did?"

"I wanted to spend a few days in the bookstores around the University of Chicago." Samuel looked at his drink. "We would have flown back together."

"So you were in Chicago when all these events took place?"

"Yes, I was in Chicago."

36 DR. JACK O'KELLY HAD TAKEN HIS own room in the Morris Inn, but the fact that his daughter was rooming with his wife could have been explanation enough of that. Couples of an age can bear a little separation. But the separation of the O'Kellys was the effect of will and not merely of time. When Maureen went to her husband's room those who knew her well would have been surprised at her trepidation and the timidity with which she tapped upon his door.

"It's open," cried a muffled voice, and Maureen entered.

The doctor was on the phone and made the usual gestures to explain, excuse, yet to continue attending to someone elsewhere. He turned away from Maureen as he ended the call a minute later.

"Well," he said, facing her.

"You missed the funeral."

"I came down to offer you my moral support, at Francie's request. A detective named Stewart phoned me several times."

"They think I killed Mortimer Sadler."

"What nonsense! I want to talk with Stewart. I'll put the fear of God into him."

"You're being very gallant."

"Would you rather I hadn't come?"

"Jack . . ." She moved toward him and he gripped her upper arms, more in defense than in an embrace. She stepped back. "Well, it gives you a chance to see your alma mater."

He looked at the windows. "I scarcely recognized a thing."

"Let's go for a walk."

"A walk?"

"About the campus. Don't you advise patients to exercise? Heal thyself."

His smile dimmed at this scriptural note. Despite Maureen's wandering being the original cause of their estrangement, it was now understood, at least by her, that the separation was his doing. His chin lifted.

"Okay. I'll change shoes."

As they went through the lobby they ran into Francie and Vivian, and the girls showed too obvious a delight at seeing the O'Kellys together.

"Where have you been?"

"Out. Everywhere. We stopped at the Grotto."

"There's our destination," Maureen said brightly to her husband, putting her arm through his. Francie glowed as if recent prayers of hers were being answered.

Outside, they turned north and strolled toward the Main Building and at once the campus of their youth seemed all around them. When he stopped at a bench to retie his sneakers, Maureen sat beside him and put a hand on his shoulder.

"It was all so long ago."

He glanced at her, looked in her eyes and nodded. "A very long time ago. Did you attend Sadler's funeral?"

"Of course I did."

"Of course."

"Oh, Jack." Her hand slid down his arm but he took it and pulled her to her feet. "We're out for a walk, remember."

And so they walked in silence around the basilica and did go down the steps to the Grotto. Many alumni entertain the pleasantly false memory that they often visited this replica of the grotto at Lourdes, a sign of the fierce Marian devotion of Father Edward Sorin, the university's founder. It was not the frequency of visits that imprinted the place on one's memory but its open-air unapologetic tribute to the Mother of God, Notre Dame. Maureen was almost surprised when Jack went directly to one of the prie-dieux and knelt. She stood beside him. He seemed to be praying. But for what did he pray? The thought was not reassuring. She knelt beside him.

They had been married in the basilica and afterward had come here, Jack in his wedding suit, she in her bridal dress, and knelt like this. Maureen's eyes swam with tears as she remembered the hope and excitement of that day. And the feeling of triumph. She had won Jack away from Laura Kennedy, the woman to whom he had been informally engaged. Now she had the terrible suspicion that it was Laura he prayed for, Laura and freedom from her and a new life before him, at his age! It was ridiculous. She stood and waited until he stood, too. He turned and looked toward the lake.

"Shall we?"

"Yes!"

And so around St. Mary's Lake they went, side by side, talk unnecessary because of the constant distraction of ducks and the sweet aroma of flowers. The path was not the makeshift one of long ago, but a firm and tended route that kept close to the shore.

They were halfway around, below Fatima Retreat House, when Maureen stopped. She waited until he faced her.

"Jack, I want this separation to end."

He considered her as an adult would a child. "It's a little late for that."

"Nonsense. Nothing has happened."

"Nothing?"

"You know what I mean. It is a trial, that's all. Come home, Jack."

They stood in silence for a time and then he took her hand, but it was not, she thought for a wild moment, a gesture of reconciliation. He talked as if to himself, explaining that he had treated Laura Kennedy shabbily once before and he didn't intend to repeat that act.

"We have had our years together, Maureen. Many of them good. The children are raised. Who knows how much time we have left? You may think you miss me, but I know you better than that. Maybe I should have let you make the first move."

"I would never have done that."

"Perhaps not. But things have been done." He looked at her. "Things that can't be undone."

"Think of Francie."

"I do. Children of failed marriages have a strong incentive not to repeat the sins of their parents."

"You can't marry Laura, Jack. It would be a sin if you did."

"Maybe."

"What do you mean?"

"Surely you know how easily annulments are granted now."

"Annulments!" Suddenly she was furious. "You wouldn't do that to me. You couldn't do that to Francie. I would kill you if you tried."

It provided him with the cruelest remark of all. "Not all problems can be solved in that way, Maureen."

37 ROGER KNIGHT FOUND HIS OWN life somewhat comic, a series of chance and improbable events. Orphaned as scarcely more than a child, he had been raised by Phil, who had adamantly opposed all suggestions that they be parceled out to relatives. In the end, their Aunt Cecilia had moved into the house their parents had left them, and some semblance of a normal household was established. Cecilia was a widow whose treatment of her late husband had been legendary in the family, but in bereavement she rewrote the history of her marriage and was often to be found mooning over photograph albums, recalling the alleged idyl of her married life. Her nephews were an enigma to her, but she became devoted to them, in her way.

When she too went to God, Phil, then returned from Vietnam, established himself as a private investigator and took his younger brother under his wing. When the supposedly slow-witted Roger was discovered to have enormous talent and potential, he had scooted through high school in a year and a half and been accepted as a graduate student in philosophy at Princeton. There he had become a Catholic and prepared himself for the academic life he was never allowed to enter.

Interviews for potential jobs had been exercises in futility, the committees abashed by the range and depth of his knowledge but provided with the undeniable fact of his enormous weight to justify passing him over. And so, with the romantic notion that he would rival Phil, he had slimmed down and enlisted in the navy, where he spent a year proving that he was not meant to be a sailor. His discharge had been honorable but early and, once more a civilian, he had obtained a licence and become his brother's partner.

The vast network of computers that can put one into instantaneous contact with almost anyone else is called the World Wide Web, and Roger was soon entangled in it as a fly to its spider. Soon he was in daily communication with scholars around the globe. The success of Phil's agency gave Roger ample leisure, even when they were on cases, to go off in a van that Phil had had remodeled to accommodate his enormous girth in a swivel chair in the back, where he could plink away on his computer. It was when they were on a case in Memphis that Roger had, in the course of two weeks, written his monograph of Baron Corvo. Phil submitted it to a publisher, it knew an unexpected success, one result of which was the visit from Father Carmody offering Roger the Huneker Chair of Catholic Studies at Notre Dame.

It was because his own life was so improbable in retrospect that Roger seldom felt surprise or censure at the folly of the lives of those their investigations involved them in. But they had all been strangers. With the death of Mortimer Sadler by poisoning, he and Phil were dealing with people who were

189

friends. All Roger's efforts to free Francie O'Kelly from tragedy involved others he was almost equally loath to incriminate.

The sight of the window box in Paul Sadler's room in Morrissey had led to a discovery that seemed to divert suspicion from Francie's mother. Until he confronted Paul, that is. The young man had told him that Mrs. O'Kelly had asked for cuttings from the deadly nightshade plant he had been cultivating in his room. While he agonized over whether to tell his brother this, Paul had been taken off to Emergency where it was discovered that he too had been poisoned as his father had. Jimmy Stewart was then prompted to concentrate once more on Maureen O'Kelly as the culprit.

"But what of the poisoned water in Toolin's bag?" Roger asked.

"She must have thought he was part of Sadler's student crusade against coeducation."

"Then why not the other roommates?"

"That is a question I must put to her."

"One you might put to yourself is when those bottles were put into Sadler's and Toolin's golf bags."

Jimmy looked at him. "When?"

"They brought the bags with them, didn't they?"

"Oh, come on, Roger. Not that again."

"Jimmy, what do you have except a quarrel twenty-five years in the past?"

"I'll tell you." And Jimmy reviewed the exchange between Mortimer Sadler and Maureen at the Sorin Restaurant in the Morris Inn.

"When Sadler's companions disavowed any connection with his student campaign?"

"You think she believed that?"

It would have been easier for Roger to speak of the flimsiness of Jimmy Stewart's suspicions if he had not been told by Paul that Maureen was in possession of cuttings of deadly nightshade, a plant she knew well, having grown it in her herb garden in Minneapolis. Finally, Roger told Phil of Samuel's having been in nearby Chicago during the tragic events on campus.

"It's not much more than an hour's drive away, Phil."

"You think he killed his brother?"

"Remember Cain and Abel."

"And his son?"

But Roger had thought of that. "Paul could have administered the poison to himself."

"Roger, you can't just pick up deadly nightshade at your local florist."

"He wouldn't have to."

Phil listened, stunned, while Roger told him of his visit to Paul's room. "Why the hell didn't you tell me this before?" he said when Roger had finished.

"For the same reason I have kept silent about Samuel Sadler."

"And what is that?"

"Francie."

Phil thought about that, and while he understood Roger's tangled motivation he was no less angry. That was when Roger should have told his brother that Maureen O'Kelly had gotten cuttings for Paul's plant before Mortimer Sadler's fatal final round on the front nine of Burke. But before he could, Phil stormed out of the apartment and drove off to talk to Jimmy Stewart.

JIMMY STEWART HAD TALKED WITH
Samuel Sadler, an exchange of a few
words, during which he assured the man that they would find
who murdered his brother.

"Then you're sure it was murder?"

"There are only two possibilities. Suicide was a possibility
only so long as we didn't know that others had been put in
danger in the same way."

"His classmate Toolin?"

"That's right."

And that was it, save for some questions about the kind of
man his brother was.

"The pillar of the family. That enabled me to live the kind
of life I prefer."

"And now?"

"I will keep the seat warm for Paul."

When Phil Knight gave him the information about
Samuel's being in Chicago and not far off in Minneapolis as
had been thought, it seemed worth looking into. Jimmy had no
more stomach for accusing Maureen O'Kelly than the Knight
brothers apparently had.

"Could you check it out, Phil?"

"So you've met my brother," Phil said when he had been admitted to Samuel Sadler's room. A laptop computer was on the desk surrounded by books, and Phil had obviously interrupted a man at work.

"I hope to see him again before I leave."

"When will that be?"

"I won't go until Paul has been released from the hospital. My schedule is pretty much what I decide it is."

"You're retired."

"From teaching, yes. For years I have been dreaming of writing a book on critics of the Enlightenment: de Maistre, Chateaubriand . . ."

Phil held up a hand. "That's Roger's department. You would be surprised how little I know."

"I understand you're a detective."

"Semiretired. My schedule, too, is what I make it. The university asked me to keep close to the investigation of your brother's death."

"Stewart seemed to think I am eager to have the culprit found."

"Aren't you?"

"Would it really make any difference?"

"Stewart is a cop, not a philosopher. Of course he intends to solve this case."

"Has he made much progress?"

"A little." Phil crossed his legs. "Roger enjoyed talking with you."

"I shall want to try out on him some of the themes of my book. I suppose it is a what-if theory. What if the contemporary criticisms of the Enlightenment and the French Revolution had become the dominant view."

Again Phil displayed a protective hand. "You were doing research in Chicago?"

"That's right."

"Where?"

"The Newberry Library."

"Where is that?"

"Your brother would know."

But Phil got the location from Samuel Sadler. He did not want Roger to know that he was on this wild goose chase as a favor to Jimmy Stewart. It proved to be a wild goose chase indeed.

Phil took the South Shore to Chicago and then a cab to the Newberry Library where, as he had hoped, a book was kept of those who made use of the facilities there. The woman he talked to, Maud Gonne, seemed an historical specimen herself, seventyish, dim eyed. She worked her lips as she studied the visitor's book.

"Samuel Sadler," Phil reminded her.

"My hearing is perfectly in order," she said primly. She was turning pages. "How long ago would this have been?"

Phil told her. She turned back a page or two, then looked up at him.

"I don't find his name here." Belatedly, she wondered what the basis of this inquiry was. "Why are you asking?"

"My brother often comes here. Roger Knight."

"Roger Knight!" Her thin lips widened to display a row of too-even teeth. "He is your brother?" She looked at Phil in disbelief.

"He got all the fat in the family."

"He is just the size he should be. The British have a saying, meant as praise: 'A man has bottom.' It fits your brother perfectly."

"We had a special chair made for his study at home."

Maud Gonne blushed. "That isn't what the phrase means." She hesitated. "It is a metaphor."

"Could Samuel Sadler have used the library without signing in?"

"Oh no. It is an ironclad rule. Is your brother with you?"

She seemed disappointed to learn that Roger was not in Chicago. Phil managed to get away without indicating his surprise that Samuel Sadler's account of his time in Chicago could not be corroborated.

From the Newberry, Phil went to police headquarters, where an old acquaintance, Parker Nosey, agreed to check out the registrations at Chicago hotels for the days Samuel said he had been in the city.

"That's hackwork, Phil, as you know. I'll put someone on it. Meanwhile, what do you say to lunch at Berghoff's?"

The prospect of the restaurant's legendary sauerkraut made Phil leap at the invitation. For the next two hours, he and Nosey quaffed beer and ate like starving Germans. Nosey was a White Sox fan, but Phil was made tolerant by the Berghoff's heavy fare and he listened to the captain's hopes for the current season. He nursed in silence his own persistent if often dashed hopes for the Cubs. By the time they returned to Nosey's office, the report was ready.

"Zilch," said Nosey. "We tried the hotels near the Newberry and then did a citywide search. No Samuel Sadler. What's it all about?"

"Just routine."

Nosey narrowed his eyes. "Wasn't someone named Sadler found dead on the golf course at Notre Dame?"

"This is his brother."

Nosey did not pursue it because he was interrupted by the ringing of his phone. Phil rose to go, pantomiming his thanks and heading for the door. By the time he looked back as he closed the door, Nosey had swung toward the window and was deep in conversation.

On the jolting train ride back to South Bend, Phil got out his cell phone several times, but he returned it to his pocket without using it. Jimmy must be told of what he had learned, however tangential the information was to his investigation. But Phil wanted to talk to Roger first.

In South Bend, trains, planes, automobiles, and buses all arrive at the airport. Phil caught a cab and was taken to the campus and the apartment he shared with Roger. When he came in, he was surprised to find Roger deep in conversation with Samuel Sadler. He greeted the two and beat it into the kitchen for a beer. Their voices came to him, the topic some essay on the French Revolution by an Italian named Manzoni. Phil went on to his own room and picked up the phone, then decided not to call Jimmy Stewart. No doubt there was a simple explanation for Samuel Sadler's whereabouts when his brother was poisoned at Notre Dame. Surely Jimmy didn't imagine that Samuel was the murderer.

That was when Phil decided to take up what might have been Jimmy's suggestion had he learned that Phil had drawn a blank in Chicago. He called Michigan City, the town he had just passed through when returning on the South Shore, and had Henry Wales, another professional friend and a chief of detectives, run a similar check of hotels in Michigan City. Within an hour the answer came. Nothing.

"Call the major motel chains, Phil. They have common records."

"Good idea. Thanks."

"This have to do with the murder at Notre Dame?"

Wales was an alumnus of Indiana University, which may have accounted for the edge in his voice when he mentioned Notre Dame.

"Indirectly. Maybe."

None of the major chains had accommodated Samuel Sadler during the relevant days. Phil sat in puzzlement. From Roger's study, the discussion continued. Reluctant to break it up, Phil pursued a wild possibility and put through a call to Niles, Michigan, a town just seven miles to the north. He spoke to another detective friend, Carl Bristol, who said he would check it out.

While he waited, Phil heard Roger's shuffling approach and then he was in the doorway. "Had a nap?"

"Has he gone?"

"No, no. Why don't you join us, Phil?"

"It's all over my head."

"No, it's over mine. He wants to talk baseball."

And so it was that Phil was deep in a discussion of the Minnesota Twins when the phone rang. Roger answered it and called out.

"It's for you, Phil. Detective Wales from Niles."

Phil took the call in the kitchen.

"You said Samuel Sadler, Phil?"

"Any luck?"

"He stayed at the Wildflower Motel for three days." He gave the dates.

"Thanks, Carl."

"He any relation of the guy who was killed?"

"His brother."

"Keep me posted, Phil."

Phil put down the phone and waited a minute before going back to the study. While he had been talking baseball with Samuel Sadler, all the puzzlement of his trip to Chicago had dissipated. How could so knowledgeable a fan come under suspicion? When he emerged, Roger and his guest were at the door.

"I'm going to give him a ride back to the Morris Inn, Phil."

"Nonsense. I'll take him. You're going to make our supper, aren't you?"

And so it was arranged. Samuel got settled beside him on the seat of the golf cart and Phil set off.

"You had a call from Niles," Samuel said quietly.

"I went up to Chicago. To the Newberry Library."

"And found I hadn't been there?"

"You were staying in Niles."

Samuel nodded. "The Newberry seemed a more plausible explanation. Often I find a motel room conducive to work. That's what I was doing in Niles."

Phil let it go. He was grateful that Samuel knew that his story had been looked into and been found wanting. The rest was up to Jimmy Stewart.

39 JIMMY STEWART NOW SEEMED TO have a choice between Maureen O'Kelly and Samuel Sadler as chief suspect, with some reluctance. He was still inclined toward Maureen. There was the long-standing quarrel between her and Mortimer Sadler. If it had only been something that happened years ago when they were undergraduates, the motive would have been less than weak. But what he had learned about the exchanges between the two the day before Sadler turned up dead—the bet on their golf game, his anger at Maureen for showing up at the closed alumni reunion he had planned—brought the whole thing into the present.

Over and above motive, there was the question of means. The poison that had killed Sadler came from a kind of plant that Maureen O'Kelly cultivated in her Minneapolis garden. But there was still the matter of opportunity. How would Maureen have put a bottle of poisoned water in Sadler's bag, betting that he would swill it down even during an early-morning round? That difficulty had been overcome when Stewart had a talk with Swannie, the head of the grounds crew at Burke.

"Is it always this cool in here?" he asked Swannie. The low

shed had doors on the north and south sides and they were wide open, allowing a breeze off the lake to pass through.

"This is nothing. In the morning I have to wear a jacket."

"How early do you begin?"

"We do the greens in first light, long before anyone shows up."

"Who's we?"

"I have a crew of three."

"They all do greens?"

Swannie made a grunting sound. "I do the greens myself. Try to get anyone to show up before seven o'clock."

"You do them yourself?"

"I enjoy it. And I want it done right." His sad look grew sadder. "Who knows how long before they build on *this* nine."

It emerged that Swannie had been cutting the greens the morning Sadler was killed.

"I start on nine and work backward."

"You saw him start off?"

"I saw you and Phil Knight drive off one." Swannie smiled and Jimmy remembered his skied drive that had gone but fifty yards. "I was already on the eighth green."

"You see the guy who started after us?"

"I thought it was a twosome. Him and his wife."

"Why would you think that?"

"I saw her come into the shelter behind the first tee. He was down practicing putting. He was already there when I did the ninth green."

"You saw a woman in the shelter."

"She came out and went to the cart the guy I thought was

her husband had gotten ready before he went to the practice putting green."

"His clubs on the cart?"

Swannie nodded. "All he needed was his putter."

"I don't suppose you got a good look at her from the eighth green."

"A blonde."

"You sure?"

"When she came out of the shelter the sun hit her hair. Quite a dish she seemed, even from that distance."

"When we got to the sixth green it hadn't been mown. It was dewy like all the others."

Swannie looked sheepish. "I was concentrating on what I was doing but the next time I looked he was heading for the second green in the cart. Alone. Naturally I wondered what had happened to the woman."

"Naturally."

"I could always finish the greens."

"You're in charge. What did you do?"

"I walked back along the ninth fairway when you and Knight had gone to the second tee. When I got back to the shelter, there was no sign of her. I went down to the practice green, but she wasn't there, either. So I came in here for a cup of coffee."

All this had been established before Phil passed on the information about Samuel Sadler's stay in the Niles motel. Jimmy decided to check out the brother before he confronted Maureen with what he had learned about her early morning appearance at the starter's shelter on the first tee and the fact that she had been seen at Sadler's cart while he was on the practice putting green. If nothing else, it would give him time to decide how to handle her.

"You gathered the information, Phil. Come on with me when I talk to him."

It was Jimmy's plan to question Samuel conspicuously in the lobby of the Morris Inn so that if Maureen noticed, she wouldn't realize that she was still his primary suspect. When Samuel came down to the lobby in response to Jimmy's call, his son Paul was with him.

"You're out of the hospital?" Jimmy said.

"I'm fine."

Samuel looked from Phil to Jimmy after they had taken seats in the lobby. "So you've learned that I was in the vicinity when Mort died?"

"In Niles."

"That's right."

It was Paul who reacted. "What is this, anyway?"

"Just a few routine questions."

"Don't give me that crap. I warn you not to try to pin this on my father."

"Paul," his father said gently. "No one has suggested such a thing."

"They better not. Look, Lieutenant, I'll give you a hint. Take a look in Mrs. O'Kelly's golf bag."

"Why would I do that?"

"Just take a look!"

"You think there's a bottle of poisoned water in her bag, too?"

"It's in the trunk of her car out in the parking lot."

"You're sure of that?"

"Paul," his father began, but his son was on his feet.

"Why don't we check?"

"Break into her car?"

Paul seemed not to have considered this problem, but as soon as he did he had a solution. "I'll call Francie."

And off he went to the house phone at the front desk. Samuel looked at Jimmy and Phil apologetically. "He seems to think I need protection."

"Tell me about your relations with your brother."

Samuel sat back in silence for a moment. "I suppose you have to ask me these things. Very well."

And he told Jimmy and Phil what they already knew about the primary role that Mortimer had assumed in the family business as well as in the Sadler Foundation.

"I know Paul thought that I was being slighted. Perhaps from time to time I was a little irked to be treated like the village idiot whenever anything practical was at stake. But the truth was I was relieved that Mort assumed the primary responsibility. It left me free for my own pursuits. After my wife died, I was even more grateful not to have to concern myself with business or the work of the foundation. Paul effectively became my proxy at meetings."

Paul joined them, accompanied by a puzzled Francie.

"What is it?" she asked.

"Francie, they want to see your mother's golf bag."

"What?" She stepped away from Paul.

"It's just routine," Paul said, looking to Jimmy for help.

Francie turned to Jimmy Stewart. "Lieutenant, I want you to stop harassing my mother. Oh, I know what you're after with all these questions. Where did you get the idea of looking at her golf bag?"

All heads turned toward Paul, and Francie's mouth opened as she stared at him. She turned to Jimmy Stewart.

"All right. Let's go look at her golf bag."

And she marched across the lobby to the entrance and the others fell into step behind her. Samuel put his arm around Paul's shoulders.

Francie was already at the car when they came into the parking lot. She got a key into the trunk and turned it. Slowly the door lifted. She stepped aside and waited for Jimmy Stewart. But it was Paul who got the bag out of the trunk and stood it up against the back bumper. Jimmy made a thorough search, unzipping pockets, taking out gloves and balls and tees. He then removed the clubs and examined the main compartment of the bag. He looked at Paul.

"Nothing."

Francie glared at Paul. "What did you think they would find?"

But Paul had pushed Jimmy aside and was searching the bag himself. Francie watched him with angry eyes, but there was the beginning of a smile on her lips.

40 THAT EVENING PHIL WAS RECOUNT-
ing these odd events to Roger when there
was a knock on the door. It was Francie O'Kelly.

"There's something I have to tell you," she said to Phil
when she had come in.

This was unusual. Phil usually felt like a spear carrier,
someone all but invisible in the background, when Francie
visited.

"What is it?"

"Now I know who put the plastic bag of deadly nightshade
in my mother's golf bag. Paul Sadler!"

"What plastic bag?"

"The one Paul thought you would find." Her eyes went to
Roger. "I've done a very stupid thing, thank God."

The two brothers listened to her account of taking her
mother's bag to practice on what was left of the old sixteenth
fairway.

"You can imagine what I thought when I found it." She
looked abject. "But now I know how it got there."

"You buried it?" Phil said.

"Yes! What if I hadn't? You and Lieutenant Stewart would

have thought just what Paul wanted you to think. What an awful thing for him to do."

Roger had sat round eyed through her recitation. Now he began to rock back and forth on the center cushion of the couch.

"Protecting his father?"

"Why do you suppose he led Jimmy Stewart and Phil out to your mother's car? To lead them away from his father."

"But he came along."

"You know what I mean."

For the first time she sat, falling into a chair as if she had been dropped. "He thinks his father is guilty?"

She fell silent and the anger she had been feeling toward Paul seemed to melt away. It would be difficult for her to forget what Paul had attempted to do to her mother, but this explanation made them oddly allies, children protecting their parents.

"That's nuts," Phil said.

"Why?" Francie asked sharply.

In a ruminative voice, Roger outlined what he assumed to be Paul's thinking. Paul attributed to his father the resentment of Mortimer Sadler that he himself felt. Mortimer Sadler Hall, so equivocally named, represented Mortimer seeking to take sole credit for his family's generosity in providing the building to Notre Dame. How could his father not secretly seethe as he contemplated the usurpations of his younger brother? Samuel's secretive presence in the neighborhood when his brother was poisoned enabled Paul to leap to the conclusion that it was his father who had put the bottle of poisoned water in Mortimer's golf bag, intending the result that had in fact occurred.

"I still say it's nuts," Phil said.

"Of course there is another explanation."

"What?" Francie sat up at the suggestion.

But Roger was slow to answer and when he did his voice had dropped a register. "He could have been diverting suspicion from himself."

"But Paul was poisoned, too."

"Yet you are sure he planted a plastic bag of deadly nightshade in your mother's golf bag."

"He had to."

Phil was on his feet. "Come show me where you buried it."

They went together, all three, Phil at the wheel of the golf cart, Roger squeezed into the seat beside him, Francie in back, riding side saddle, as it were, and leaning forward between the two brothers.

The sun was a red disc in the western sky when they turned onto the Burke golf course, went up past the tiled drinking fountain and out on the ninth fairway. The course was deserted now, and the hum of insects was beginning to give way to the chirp of their nocturnal counterparts. Birds made lazy swings through the sky, the penultimate swoops before the sun would suddenly drop from sight and twilight come on.

Francie directed Phil to the black metal fence that separated the remnant of the sixteenth fairway from Cedar Grove Cemetery. It took a while before she located the spot. She clambered out of the cart and knelt, pulling away clumps of dirt tufted with grass. She turned, holding up the plastic bag.

209

It was Roger who took it from her, holding it up so that the rays of the setting sun made the plastic shine and brought out the colors of its contents. He nodded. "How did you know what it was, Francie?"

"I've seen the plant at home."

"Did you notice it in the window box in Paul's room?"

"Is that why we went there?"

"I suppose it could have been determined whether these came from his plant."

"Could have been?"

"The window box is now gone."

"It had to come from there."

Phil had been listening impatiently. "But why did he put it in Mrs. O'Kelly's golf bag?"

"For the same reason he led you and Jimmy to her car."

"To divert suspicion from his father?"

"Or from himself." Roger's words seemed to lift like smoke into the suddenly twilit air. Beyond the fence, in Cedar Grove, a figure stood motionless beside a grave, wholly unaware of the trio on the fairway.

"Jimmy has to be told," Phil said. They were all three back in the cart. He turned the key and they rolled silently away across the grassy expanse.

CAL SWITHINS CONTINUED TO stand motionless beside the grave, his head bowed as it had been while he watched the girl dig beside the fence. A small smile played on his thin lips. He had witnessed their exodus from the Morris Inn some time before and watched without comprehending what took place when the trunk of a parked car was opened and a golf bag extracted. When Phil went to the Knight apartment, Swithins had followed, not even trying to formulate to himself his reason for doing so. He was seated on a bench, keeping vigil, when the girl arrived. He recognized her then, as he had not in the parking lot of the Morris Inn. The daughter of Maureen O'Kelly. When the three emerged from the apartment and set off, he followed at a discreet distance, easily keeping the slow-moving cart within sight. When they arrived at the golf course, he followed along the outer road to the cemetery and then took up his station beside a randomly chosen grave.

Now, he walked slowly to his own car in the parking lot of the Morris Inn, letting what he had seen over the past hours move across the screen of memory uninterpreted, not forcing an explanation. That, he was confident, would come.

He was settled behind the wheel when the cell phone in his

pocket rang, causing him to yelp. He felt like a parolee under electronic surveillance. It was Maddie Yost.

"Where's your column? We're going to press."

Her barking voice induced the guilt it was meant to. His first defense was a lie.

"Check your e-mail, Maddie."

"You sent it in?"

"I'll resend it when I get home."

"Keep it short. I don't have time to whittle it down to size."

Profanity was not a prominent element in Cal Swithins's linguistic repertoire, but on such occasions he could summon from the byways of memory, and most recent films, the requisite words. He was still sitting in his parked car in the lot of the Morris Inn when he spoke aloud of Maddie Yost as no woman has ever been spoken of before, at least by Cal Swithins. Something caused him to turn and see in the next car an elderly lady staring at him with bright and startled eyes. He hadn't noticed her before. What was she doing, just sitting there in a parked car? Had she been abandoned? In any case, he had obviously shocked her sensibilities.

"I beg your pardon," he called across the gap between the cars.

"What?"

"I said I'm sorry."

She nodded her head in comprehension. "In a few minutes."

"I had no idea you were there."

"Yes, I think so."

She was deaf as a post. He smiled at her and she frowned

212

back. He started his car and backed away. He could have gone on with impunity consigning Maddie Yost to the infernal regions. Ah well, iratus interruptus. But wrath returned as he recalled her suggestion that she must edit what he wrote. He felt like a missionary among savages; he was perhaps the only literate person on the staff of *The Shopper*. This was cause for shame rather than pride. How in God's name had he sunk so low?

This familiar thought was more tolerable now because of the promise the Sadler story held for bringing about a dramatic turn in his career. He would take a first pass at writing the story as soon as he got home. Appearance in *The Shopper* scarcely counted as publication. His dry run at an account of the strange happenings on the Notre Dame campus would doubtless go unread. Maddie would only count the words, not read them. Cal Swithins would be limbering up for the quantum jump into the pages of the *Chicago Tribune*.

At home, restored with a TV dinner, he sat at his laptop in that holy moment before composition begins. The world and its allurements fell out of consciousness, a small pinpoint of light far down the tunnel of his mind grew in size, absorbing him into it. His fingers began to move upon the keys: "It was the best of times, it was the worst of times . . ." He stopped. No. Something else. "All unhappy families are alike but the Sadler family is unique." Ah. Better. His fingers began to move more rapidly over the keyboard of his computer and he seemed literally inspired as he wrote.

He had written a hundred words when the screen went blank. He yelped as if in physical pain. The battery was depleted; he had not plugged in the laptop when he sat down to work. That lovely beginning was lost! But minutes later, wired and fired up, his fingers flew across the keyboard as what he had previously written came back to him verbatim. It was difficult not to stop and send up a prayer of thanksgiving.

42 WHEN SAMUEL PASSED DR. O'KELLY
on the way into the dining room, he
merely bowed and went on. Nor did O'Kelly show any inclination to exceed mere civility. The fact was that neither man
really knew the other; they were connected only through a
common acquaintance with Laura Kennedy. Acquaintance.
What a quaint way of putting it. Samuel took\ a table near the
window and looked out at a squirrel busy on the lawn. The old
sadness descended, pushing away his reaction to the awful
events of recent days.

Over the past year he had come to love Laura Kennedy.
Late at night, in his condo by the lake, he wrote poetry for her,
in pencil in an examination booklet, one of the dozens brought
with him from the college where he had taught. It did not matter that the poetry was bad. Writing it was a species of ther-
apy. Of course he never showed it to her. His reluctance had a
double source.

The first was the sense of disloyalty he felt to his late wife
to be mooning over a woman as old as himself, however better
preserved. Laura Kennedy had never married but she was the
most matronly and aristocratic woman Samuel had ever seen.

The sight of her stirred him as nothing had since his bereavement.

The second source was his habitual lack of self-confidence. Like so many others, he had been attracted to the academic life by its implicit promise that the inchoate years of adolescence could be indefinitely prolonged. It was like declaring oneself neutral in the battle of life. His had been a modest career on a mediocre campus. Seldom had he ignited in students his own passion for the authors they read. Over the years, he realized he had become a figure of fun as a teacher. Nothing malicious, just the cruel condescension of youth for age. His own youth had ended when his wife died and the stable point of reference of home and family was gone. Paul had been twelve when his mother died. It seemed to mature him. Such continuity as there was between his earlier life and now was provided by Paul. Never before had Samuel felt so thoroughly that his life was a failure. Everything Paul said or did announced his belief that his father was a failure.

As I suppose I am, Samuel conceded to himself. As success is judged by Mortimer and Paul, I am a failure. He retired early and took up his solitary life on the shore of Lake Minnetonka. It was when he had reluctantly responded to the importuning of his pastor and given a weekday evening talk to a handful of people on *Moby Dick* that Laura Kennedy came up to thank him afterward.

"You make me want to read it again."

"So you have read it."

"Oh yes." Her head turned slightly but her eyes remained on him. "You realize that I have known you forever."

He stepped back as if he needed a better look. From any vantage point she was an impressive woman.

"Laura Kennedy. St. Mary's '74."

"Good grief. I wish I could say I recognize you."

"I wouldn't believe you if you did."

They went off together for coffee in a little place in Wayzata, he following her car in his. A first encounter between two people who had known one another, however imperfectly, so long ago, is necessarily spent in filling the gaps. Samuel surprised himself when he told her he had lost his wife.

"I'm sorry. I never married."

"So what do you do?"

A wry smile. "Manage money."

He thought it was her job, but she meant she looked after the Kennedy money. "You could say I husband it. God knows I often feel married to it."

On the way home it occurred to him that he had been at ease with her from the first moment that she came forward after his talk. Their conversation at the coffee shop had been similarly smooth. She was the first woman he had really talked with since his wife died. Their subsequent get-togethers brought back the excitement of college days, talking about what one was reading, each of them unbound by any of the usual ties that bind those their age. He could not understand why she had never married. Surely men in number must have come pounding on her door. One night he dreamt first of his wife, then of Laura, and it was as if he was being given permission to be bold. It was the following day that he saw Laura with O'Kelly.

It was in the restaurant in Wayzata, one Samuel had come

to think of as theirs. Laura was even sitting at the table they had shared, her winsome smile turned now on O'Kelly. Samuel turned and left the restaurant. That night he burned all the silly poetry he had written. He sat up late sipping scotch and water and apologized to his dead wife, as if she could care that he was such a fool. It hurt him to realize that O'Kelly was a far more fitting match for Laura, a head taller with thick, silver hair and an expression that seemed the end or the beginning of a smile. When Samuel heard that Jack had taken a swing at Mort for an ungentlemanly remark, he wanted to call Laura and dissociate himself from his brother's words.

Learning that O'Kelly was married had slowed Samuel's sense that he had been replaced. After Mass one Sunday, he ran into Laura and they talked brightly on the sidewalk outside and he felt the faint stir of hope.

"Do you know Jack O'Kelly?" she asked.

"The doctor."

"You were classmates, you know."

"I didn't know."

"We all were, if you'll count St. Mary's."

"Did you know him then?"

Cool gray eyes moved across the middle distance and came to rest on him. "Yes."

That one word was enough. The details he got, whether he wanted them or not, from Mortimer. Laura and O'Kelly had been engaged, more or less informally. She wore his class ring. But a freshman named Maureen had put an end to that.

"So she never married," Mort concluded.

"Brokenhearted?"

"After all these years, he would like to mend it."

"But he's married."

"Not for long."

"I don't believe Laura Kennedy would ever marry a divorced man. She's Catholic through and through."

"You may be right."

43 DENNIS GRANTLEY WAS SITTING
in Father Carmody's room in Holy Cross
House nursing a gill of Powers while the old priest talked on
the phone to Phil Knight. Grantley would have felt like an
eavesdropper if the old priest's voice did not carry to the
nurses' station and beyond. If Carmody spoke that loudly in
the confessional he would bring back public penance.

"Nonsense," Carmody shouted. "Have you talked to the
man? All right. He's incapable of such a thing."

He hummed as he listened, frowning at what he heard. He
began to nod. "Of course. It has to be her. She's the one."

When he hung up he looked at Grantley as if he had snuck
in uninvited. Grantley lifted his glass; its moisture all that was
left of the tot the priest had poured.

"Have another." Carmody nodded toward the bottle.

"And for yourself, Father?" Grantley said, already on his
feet and gripping the bottle.

"No, no. I have it here for friends. And visitors," he added,
as if making a subtle distinction.

"How goes the investigation?"

"It's over. It's that woman. If he were still alive Mortimer would claim she proves his case against women at Notre Dame."

"Mrs. O'Kelly?"

"Guilty as sin, however provoked by that idiot Mortimer Sadler. Of course, even if found guilty, she will be out in a year or so. Even the pope is waffling on capital punishment."

How bloodthirsty Carmody seemed. Of course, it was all abstract. His single great emotion was loyalty to Notre Dame, and the events that had disturbed the campus in recent days were all viewed in the light of their effect on the university. Grantley could both see the narrowness of the point of view and share it.

"Well, you have to be on your way," Carmody announced abruptly, reaching for Grantley's glass. Grantley immediately brought it to his lips and drained the contents, lest he be robbed of the whiskey. He stood and handed over the glass. Carmody came with him to the door and then outside, where they stood in the cool of the evening, a sky full of stars above.

"Peaceful," Grantley said.

"Every man in this house would prefer commotion to peace."

"Sound the fire alarm."

"What?"

"They're bored in the firehouse, too. They'd like a little commotion."

"A false alarm?"

"Half of them are."

"Bah."

Carmody turned and went back inside. Grantley took the long way to the firehouse and his lonely room on its second floor. He thought of Agnes, felt a twinge of remorse seasoned with desire. He almost wished he had earned the guilt he felt, wished he had risen from the couch and knocked on her bedroom door. For all her flirtiness, she probably would have called the police if he responded to her tireless come-ons. A false alarm.

At the firehouse, he did not go upstairs but to his car parked in the crescent of Flanner Hall. He stopped at the Morris Inn to verify that this was indeed Agnes's night off.

"She was looking for you," Willa the butterball said, insinuation in her voice. Had Agnes been indiscreet and regaled her fellow waitresses with the story of his night on her couch? "She's in there." Willa pointed to the bar.

Habitués of bars grow used to the dim and kindly lighting. They were silhouettes at best to Grantley. His name was called, but not by Agnes. He smiled into the darkness, stopped at the bar, and ordered a scotch and water. Be you Dewars of the word and not hearers only. Shame on him. He turned and made out the grinning face of Armitage Shanks, who had called his name. Agnes sat with him at a table. She beckoned to him and he moved, helpless, toward the Siren.

"My night off," she said brightly.

"And mine on," Shanks said, and then look horrified at what he had said. Grantley sat.

"How's the arthritis?" But Shanks had taken himself from the game by his ambiguous remark, no matter that Agnes had laughed. To her Grantley said, "Willa said you were asking for me."

"Willa," Agnes said with mock disgust, but a simpering smile played on her painted lips.

"Suspicion has settled on Maureen O'Kelly."

"Shhh," Agnes said, laying a hand on his arm and tilting her head. And then Grantley saw Maureen O'Kelly at a corner table with Toolin.

44 GRANTLEY'S REMARK REACHED them at their corner table and Toolin took Maureen's hand.

"It's true," she said. "They think I did it."

"They think *I* did it."

"Not any more."

"Tell me about it."

How matter-of-fact she sounded, ticking off the case against herself. Francie's certainty that Paul Sadler had planted the plastic bag of deadly nightshade in her golf bag was dismissed as a daughter's loyalty.

"So how did it get there?"

"God only knows."

"Someone put it there."

"Someone?"

"Your husband?"

She smiled. "He doesn't have to get rid of me. He's already left me."

"For Laura Kennedy."

"If she'll have him. I broke them up long ago and neither can forgive me now."

"What exactly have the police said?"

"I was advised to get a lawyer."

"You must. Someone has to talk sense to them."

"It's not wise of you to be seen with me."

"I'll never leave you." His hand closed over hers.

When Maureen went up to her room Francie was watching television without much interest.

"Mom, let's go home."

"They won't let me."

"Who won't let you?"

"The police very politely asked that I stay here longer."

Francie rose and took her mother in her arms and they stood for a time in silent embrace.

"Daddy was here."

"Oh."

"He stayed for fifteen minutes before he left. Maybe you should call him."

Maureen considered it. "You call him."

Francie picked up the phone and asked for her father's room. A minute passed. She hung up. "No answer."

"It's just as well."

At two in the morning Francie made another call, a frantic summons for help. Her mother was in the bathroom gagging. Two men from the firehouse came in a red pickup and thundered up to the room in rubber coats and huge boots.

"What's wrong?"

A pale Maureen looked out of the bathroom at the firemen.

"I think I've been poisoned."

45 ROGER SAT AT HIS COMPUTER
playing chess with an opponent halfway
around the world, but his mind was full of a conversation he
had had with Jacob Climacus. The botanist acted like the
defense attorney for deadly nightshade.

"If you ate the plant, or any part of it, sure, that would do
you in. But in water? I doubt an amateur could pull that off."

Was Mrs. O'Kelly less of an amateur in this sense just
because she had the plant in her garden? Climacus referred to
the skill necessary to extract the poison and mix it with water.
That was not the skill of a gardener.

"How would it be done?"

"A prescription for belladonna would make it easy."

On the screen, after ten minutes of inactivity, a move was
made. Roger smiled and began to tap on his keyboard. Check-
mate.

Roger rose, the game of chess forgotten, and walked as if in
a trance to the door. Outside, he got behind the wheel of his
golf cart, turned the cart, and moved silently off across the
campus walks to the Morris Inn.

He found Phil in the lobby, sitting in on the exchange
between Jimmy Stewart and Maureen O'Kelly. Roger sum-

moned his brother, led him past the entrance to the restaurant and outside where he eased himself into a chair. Phil sat and listened as Roger spoke, what he said suddenly casting recent events in a wholly different light.

"It should be easy to check on, Phil."

"I'll make a call immediately."

He went inside and Roger watched abstractly the antics of insects in the freighted air where the aroma from the flower beds seemed the very definition of summer. Climacus had suggested that nearly every plant is harmful to some animal species or other. Potentially. Roger rose with an effort he described as weight lifting and went inside.

Dr. O'Kelly came out of the elevator, a suit bag slung from his shoulder, a briefcase in his hand, and went to the desk. Roger joined him.

"We haven't met, Doctor. I'm Roger Knight."

O'Kelly stepped back and his incipient smile became full. He put out his hand. "Francie has told me of you."

"She is a very intelligent young lady."

"On her mother's side." But the gallant remark dimmed his smile.

"You're checking out?"

"I've stayed too long as it is. I have engaged Alex Cholis, the best lawyer in South Bend, for Maureen."

"Surely you don't think she is guilty."

"It's not what I think, I'm afraid."

"Could we talk?"

"Now?"

"Please."

He hesitated when he saw his wife with Jimmy Stewart. He crossed the lobby to her. "I've called a lawyer, Maureen. Alex Cholis."

"You're going?"

"Would you like me to stay?"

"What do you think?"

"Then I will. Professor Knight and I were going to have a little chat."

"Have you checked out?"

"It doesn't matter."

"You can stay with Francie and me."

"We'll see."

Once more outside, Roger lowered himself again into the snug but adequate chair. A large umbrella was open above the table.

"What more can I do?" O'Kelly asked as he sat. "Cholis is said to be a very good lawyer."

"You'll need one."

"I can't believe they suspect her."

"No, I don't suppose you do."

O'Kelly looked closely at Roger. "I don't understand."

"Oh, I think you do."

The doors of the inn slid open. Phil came out, and his expression told Roger all he needed to know. Once again he indulged in weight lifting. "I'll leave you to my brother, Doctor. He will explain."

Phil took the chair that Roger had vacated and Roger went inside. Jimmy Stewart was standing and Maureen wore a stunned expression. Obviously, Phil had already told Jimmy what he had learned. Roger waved to her but continued to the front entrance. He felt no sense of triumph. Maureen and her daughter would be relieved, of course, but then other emotions would come.

ALEX CHOLIS, THE LAWYER DR. O'Kelly had summoned for his wife, became his own now as the case against him was spelled out. The prescription he had written for belladonna could not be explained away by the imaginative story he concocted. It had been an easy matter for him to put the bottles of poisoned water in the golf bags of Mortimer Sadler and Toolin. They were all members of the Minikahda Club that overlooks Lake Calhoun in Minneapolis. The assistant to the pro was prompted by questioning to remember the doctor busy at a number of open lockers before Mort and Toolin had gone off to Notre Dame for their rump reunion.

"Why?" Greg Whelan asked, a word he had no problems with.

"Because his beloved would never marry a divorced man. A widower was another matter."

"But why kill Sadler and Toolin?"

"Once Maureen became the prime suspect in those crimes, he would stage her suicide. That was meant to seal her guilt."

Roger and Phil were entertaining Jimmy Stewart and Greg Whelan in the aftermath of Dr. O'Kelly's arraignment. Roger was swathed in an enormous apron and wore a baseball cap with ND emblazoned on it. He stood over the stove with steam from the kettle of pasta enveloping him.

"But Paul Sadler?" Greg brought out on the second try.

"Self-administered."

"Why?"

"Everything Paul did was meant to protect his father. He really thought his father was the murderer."

"Poor Francie."

Roger waved away the steam. His expression was a tragic mask. "Indeed."

She had gone back to Minneapolis with her mother—who was accompanied by Chris Toolin, much to Francie's dismay. She could not understand what her mother saw in Toolin.

"It's just a rebound," she had said to Roger. "She can't live without a man to lean upon."

"What woman can?"

"I'll lean on you."

"It's not the same thing."

"I hate Paul for what he did."

"Do you? Wouldn't you have done as much for your mother?"

He left her with that thought. After the horror of her father's trial, she would look on what Paul had done in a different light. He and Climacus had gone off to Purdue, where Paul was to be acquainted with the work done there on plants inimical to animals.

"Animals, vegetables, minerals," Greg said smoothly. He was with Roger in the kitchen. Phil and Jimmy Stewart were settling down to watch the Cubs.

Father Carmody had not been philosophical when he stopped by earlier, brought by Dennis Grantley.

"His degree should be revoked," the old priest growled.

"I thought you told me that not even God can undo the past."

"God didn't give him a degree."

A more surprising visitor had been Cal Swithins. He brought a copy of the *The Shopper* that had carried his story of how Maureen O'Kelly had murdered Mortimer Sadler. The story was the basis of the libel suit Maureen O'Kelly had Cholis file against the reporter. He was sheepishly proud of the commotion he had caused.

"Do you know Agnes, the waitress at the Morris Inn?"

"What about her?" Grantley snapped.

"A lovely woman. It turns out she is a fan. She has clipped all my columns from *The Shopper*."

Like Kierkegaard, Swithins had found his single reader, but Dennis Grantley did not rejoice with him. He abandoned Father Carmody and left, doubtless on his way to the Morris Inn. Swithins was happy to stay for pasta and salad.

While they ate, Roger went on and on about belladonna. "Women used it on their eyes, to dilate them, a condition thought to enhance their beauty."

"Bah," said Father Carmody.

"I could write a column on that," Swithins said.

"Better not," Roger advised.

When the fall semester opened, Francie and Paul were reconciled. Alex Cholis was indeed a good lawyer, as goodness is measured in the law. The charge against Dr. O'Kelly was reduced from murder to homicide, and the lawyer tried to depict his client as motivated by medical concerns. It was irrational enough an explanation to sway the jury, which urged clemency when they found O'Kelly guilty. Cholis, of course, intended to appeal the verdict. In November, Samuel Sadler announced his engagement to Laura Kennedy, providing Francie and Paul an occasion to lament the folly of adults.

It was Greg Whelan who remembered that Maureen O'Kelly had been seen on the first tee doing something at Mortimer Sadler's golf cart while he finished on the practicing putting green. Francie had provided Roger with the explanation.

"It was a practical joke. She put a dozen whiffle balls in his bag. She had seen him slip out of the inn when she was about to set out jogging. Guessing what he was up to, she got the whiffle balls out of her car and put them in his bag."

Swannie's crew thus had an explanation for the dozen whiffle balls someone had thrown angrily into the rough along the third fairway of the Burke golf course.